"Hard as I tried to not fall in love with you, it didn't work."

Johnny got real quiet. "Oh," he said, and Thea's heart cramped a little.

"Yeah. *Oh*. So that's the deal. If we get married, it's with the full understanding that I love you. And I'm not gonna pretend otherwise." She angled her head, trying to see his face. "How's that going down, then?"

Laughing softly, he said, "Too soon to tell. Don't know which one of us this is scarier for."

"You…want to think this over?"

"What's to think about? Other than setting a date? When's good for you?"

"I'm seven months pregnant. I'm thinking soon."

"Soon works for me. Come here," he said, his corded arms encircling her from behind, and he smelled so fresh-from-the-shower good, her eyes closed. Then a chuckle tickled her back. "You sure you don't want to get married just so we can fool around?"

Dear Reader,

By the time this book goes to print, my husband and I will have been married for thirty years. Our secret? I have no idea. Although I'm sure a shared outlook on life hasn't hurt. Not to mention a sense of humor, (We're on our fifth teenager. 'Nuff said.) And most important, being each other's best friend. For us, marriage "took" on the first try—whatever stumbling we've done along the way, at least we've each kept the other from toppling over.

However, while Johnny and Thea in *Reining in the Rancher* may be friends, the bruises left over from a pair of failed marriages still smart, boy. So they have every reason not to trust falling in love again…especially with each other! Until the cosmos conspires to link them together for life, and they're faced with the choice of making the best of things…or—this time—making things work.

I love writing "second chance" stories, because happily-ever-after is even sweeter for those who've not only stumbled and fallen, but who, like Johnny and Thea, find the courage to get back on the horse and try again.

Enjoy.

Karen

REINING IN THE RANCHER

KAREN TEMPLETON

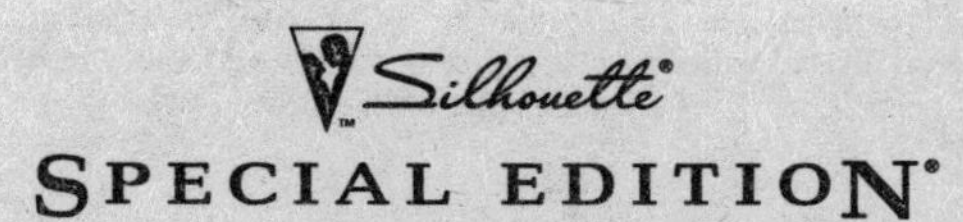

Published by Silhouette Books
America's Publisher of Contemporary Romance

ISBN-13: 978-0-373-65430-7
ISBN-10: 0-373-65430-8

Recycling programs for this product may not exist in your area.

REINING IN THE RANCHER

This edition published by arrangement with Harlequin Books S.A.

Visit Silhouette Books at www.eHarlequin.com

Printed in U.S.A.

Books by Karen Templeton

Silhouette Special Edition

Marriage, Interrupted #1721
††*Baby Steps* #1798
††*The Prodigal Valentine* #1808
††*Pride and Pregnancy* #1821
‡*Dear Santa* #1864
‡*Yours, Mine…or Ours?* #1876
‡*Baby, I'm Yours* #1893
‡‡*A Mother's Wish* #1916
‡‡*Reining in the Rancher* #1948

Silhouette Yours Truly

**Wedding Daze*
**Wedding Belle*
**Wedding? Impossible!*

Silhouette Romantic Suspense

Anything for His Children #978
Anything for Her Marriage #1006
Everything but a Husband #1050
Runaway Bridesmaid #1066
†*Plain-Jane Princess* #1096
†*Honky-Tonk Cinderella* #1120
What a Man's Gotta Do #1195
Saving Dr. Ryan #1207
Fathers and Other Strangers #1244
Staking His Claim #1267
***Everybody's Hero* #1328
***Swept Away* #1357
***A Husband's Watch* #1407

††Babies, Inc.
†How To Marry a Monarch
**The Men of Mayes County
*Weddings, Inc.
‡Guys and Daughters
‡‡Wed in the West

KAREN TEMPLETON

A Waldenbooks bestselling author and RITA® Award nominee, Karen is the mother of five sons and living proof that romance and dirty diapers are not mutually exclusive terms. An Easterner transplanted to Albuquerque, New Mexico, she spends far too much time trying to coax her garden to yield roses and produce something resembling a lawn, all the while fantasizing about a weekend alone with her husband. Or at least an uninterrupted conversation.

She loves to hear from readers, who may reach her by writing c/o Silhouette Books, 233 Broadway, Suite 1001, New York, NY 10279, or online at www.karentempleton.com.

To Jack
Although it's good to know we can each fly solo,
it's been a lot more fun this way.
Here's to thirty more.

Acknowledgments

To Wendy Morton, DVM, for her untiring patience
in the face of countless, clueless questions.

Chapter One

Staring at some long-gone hoochie's phone number etched into the stall door six inches from her nose, Thea Benedict tried, for the third time, to snap her jeans closed.

Her "fat" jeans.

FAIL.

"Thea!" Evangelista bellowed through the locked ladies' room door. "You comin' out sometime this year or what?"

"Yeah, yeah, yeah," Thea yelled to her boss, yanking down the idiotic babydoll top over her squished boobs. "Keep your shirt on!" She banged back the dented metal and tromped to the sink, where Corpse Bride glared back at her from the depths of the mottled mirror.

Can't put this off any longer, babycakes—

"I hope to hell you're not sick on account of somethin' you ate from here!"

Right. Like the smell alone of Mexican food didn't make

her gag these days. Her hands washed and dried, Thea fluffed up her pale, chin-length hair, then dug a little pot of lip gloss out of her pocket, smeared some on. Corpse Bride as beauty queen, whoo-hoo.

Palms pressed into the cool porcelain, she released a shaky sigh. Johnny was gonna have kittens that she'd waited this long. But when was the right time to tell somebody you broke up with four months before—somebody who routinely thanked God he only had one kid because that one was about to kill him—that your diaphragm hadn't fit as snugly as it should've?

She hoped to heaven he had enough sense not to think she'd gotten pregnant on purpose, but you never knew with men. Maybe she had come *this close* to loving the bozo, but string her up for the buzzards the day she stooped to trapping a man into marriage.

Into anything.

Thea squeezed shut her eyes, as if that were somehow gonna settle her stomach. She supposed she could say she hadn't known for sure, because of her irregular periods and all, but that hadn't been true for a few weeks. She'd known, all right, even if this time had felt different than the others. She just hadn't trusted, hadn't even wanted to take a pregnancy test because...because she just couldn't. Not even when it hurt to wear a bra and she nearly lost her cookies all over a customer's huevos rancheros and the smell of her own shampoo made her woozy—

"Thea! For God's sake—"

She smacked open the ladies' room door, sending Evangelista jumping back and the woman's mammoth bazooms into a jiggling frenzy. Behind fleshy eyelids, dark eyes went all slitty.

"*Dios mio,* you're gonna scare the customers!"

"And aren't you just the poster child for sympathy?" Thea muttered without heat, because Ev was just that way.

"An' I don't want you spreading germs all over the place!"

"Trust me, it's not contagious," Thea said with a pointed look, and Ev sucked in a breath and said, "No," and Thea said, "Yep," then sailed back out into the dining room, order pad at the ready, determined to remain cheerful despite the restaurant's boldly painted murals and lively mariachi music, and the brilliant New Mexican spring day outside the tall windows.

So she smiled, she joked, she held her breath as she set steaming platters of enchiladas and tamales and stuffed sopapillas in front of people she'd pretty much known her entire life, never mind that she felt like she was careening down a steep hill with no brakes. As the afternoon wore on, however, a sort of numb determination took over, that she wasn't about to let a little thing like an unplanned pregnancy with a man she should never have messed around with in the first place derail her, no sirree.

That is until, some hours later, when she pulled her middle-aged, mud-spattered Jeep Cherokee up in front of the sprawling ranch house Johnny Griego called home, and she caught sight of him astride an unfamiliar horse in the training paddock set between two horse barns, and her resolve balked like a stubborn colt not interested in being broke.

Nearly choking on the earthy, hay-and-horse-scented mountain breeze, she looked instead at the house, old and big and solid beneath the fireflies of sunlight darting through glittering piñons and shimmering, white-barked aspens. Many's the night Thea and Johnny and his teenage daughter, Rachel, had sat on the wraparound porch, watching lightning dance across the mesa or the sky burst into flame moments before the sun dropped behind a dozen layers of mountain ranges, and Thea'd catch the look of wonder on Johnny's face, even after twenty-five years, that it was all *his*.

Andy Morales, the ranch's previous owner, had been more than Johnny's first employer; he'd also given him an example of manhood that had been sorely lacking, Johnny's father having done a runner on him and his mother when Johnny was still a little kid. How Andy became Johnny's adoptive father, Thea wasn't sure, but she did know that Andy's leaving Johnny the ranch had been a dream come true for a young man who'd once called home a run-down, two-room adobe on the edge of town.

Her gaze reluctantly swerved back to horse and trainer, silhouetted against the vast blue sky—

Oh, for God's sake, girl—get on with it!

Slowly, shakily, Thea got out of the Jeep, her eyes fixed on Johnny's solid, compact body, easily commanding the sleek, powerfully built chestnut gelding, their perfectly synchronized tango smothered in a blur of fine red dust. A tan-colored cowboy hat shadowed a weathered face with the devilish, deep brown eyes of a much younger man, a mouth that could say more with a tiny quirk of the lips than most men could say in a hundred words, an image almost impossible to reconcile with the insecure boy she'd only known in passing growing up.

Johnny was too far away, and too intent on his task, to see her, but awareness crackled through her all the same, prickling her skin and wreaking all sorts of havoc with her breathing. Knowing how far he'd come, what he'd *over*come…she had to admit, all that hard-won confidence was pretty darn sexy. But get too close to that still-raw core—of the little boy whose father had abandoned him, the young man whose marriage had failed—and a lot of that confidence turned out to be nothing more than sheer determination to stay in control. Johnny had no trouble making decisions, following through on a promise, keeping his word. But risking his heart?

No damn way.

Sound familiar? said the voice, making Thea's forehead knot. What lay ahead wasn't gonna be pretty. For either of them. How other people pulled off the "friends with benefits" thing, she had no idea. Then again, maybe this was just another urban legend about modern relationships that nobody wanted to admit was a crock. In any case, it'd sure been a mistake for them, thinking that sex would be a good way to exercise—if not exorcise—all those pesky hormones without wading through a lot of sloppy emotions. At least Thea'd called a halt to their shenanigans while she still had a couple grains of common sense left, when she'd realized that she wanted more than Johnny'd ever be able to give her.

And hadn't that surprised the holy heck out of her, after all these years of being just fine on her own?

After all those years of refusing to cry over a man?

Hauling in a breath, she started toward the paddock—

"Thea!"

She spun around to see Johnny's daughter torpedoing toward her, the long-legged beauty's eyes bright with a mix of excitement and abject terror, and Thea's heart twanged, that while she may have broken up with Johnny, it hadn't been nearly so easy to sever ties with this bright, funny girl she'd grown to love with all her heart.

Who now threw herself into Thea's arms, nearly knocking her over.

"Omigosh, honey…what is it?" she asked, thinking, *Nope, still not used to the hair,* because what had once been dark and shiny and gorgeous now boasted ragged stripes of Bimbo Blonde and Kool-Aid Fruit Punch. Poor Johnny.

Rachel straightened, shoving a blond stripe behind one multipierced ear. "Didn't you get my voice mail?"

"What? Oh, no…I turned off my phone while I was at work and forgot to turn it back on again—"

The girl grabbed her hand and pulled her around to the side of the house, where Thea nearly gagged from the cloying scent of profusely blooming lilacs.

"I'm pregnant!"

"What?" Thea finally got out when she could hear over the ringing in her ears.

The fool child actually giggled. "Jesse and I are gonna have a baby!" Then, sobered, she clutched Thea's hand more tightly. "But how on earth am I gonna tell Dad? He'll *kill* me."

Yeah, but it'll knock the hair right off the radar, Thea thought, along with, *And isn't this seriously bad timing?* as the ramifications of this little announcement began to sink in. Then an image of the aforementioned boyfriend—of whom her father had never exactly been a big fan *before*—popped into her head, a big, bulky, bald dude whose favorite pastime was letting people poke needles loaded with colored ink into his body—

"You gotta help us tell Dad!"

"Uh, no, don't *think* so—"

"Pleeease, Thea? Jess'll be there, but—"

"And I haven't even seen your father in months!"

"So?"

Thea took a deep breath, trying to stay strong in the face of those pleading brown eyes. "So Jesse knows?" she said, stalling.

"Of course he knows, I told him, like, the second *I* knew. And he's totally cool with it." Right. All that tattoo ink must've leaked into the boy's brain, because that was the only way a nineteen-year-old boy was going to be "cool" with becoming a dad. "He's on his way over, in fact. So this is good, that you're here… Wait a minute." Brows dipped. "If you didn't get my message, why *are* you here?"

"I, um, had something to discuss with your dad."

Which at this rate wasn't gonna happen until the baby was Rachel's age, she mused as an engine roar announced Jesse's arrival on The Motorcycle with Hummer Delusions. As Jesse dismounted, like a slightly clumsy bull, Rachel glanced at her boyfriend, then back at Thea, finally looking like maybe there was a reason her news might turn her father homicidal. "Could it wait?"

Thea plastered a big old fake smile on her face. "Sure," she said, but only because it would be cruel to drop two bombshells on the poor man in one day. Not that she had a lot of days left—especially since she was so skinny she could hardly swallow an olive without it showing—but if she had to choose between keeping the truth from Johnny a little longer or giving him a heart attack, she'd go with Option #1, thank you.

Then Jesse came up behind Rachel, blocking out the sun, and Thea thought maybe the kid wasn't quite as okay about all of this as Rach might want to believe. Something about that terrified look in his eyes. Except then they got all icky-poo cuddly-wuddly—or at least Rachel did; Jesse looked a little stunned—and the stab of jealousy took Thea by complete surprise. Until reason returned and she thought, *Hell, at least I'm not seventeen.*

Which, oddly, wasn't nearly as much of a consolation as she might have hoped.

Especially when Johnny suddenly appeared around the corner of the house, all rampant suspicion and glowering protectiveness, mostly directed at Jesse, but with just enough *what-the-hell?* for Thea to make her feel part of things.

"What's going on?" he rumbled, and Thea nearly upchucked in the lilacs.

"You're *what?!*"

"Pregnant," Rachel repeated, and Johnny thought he couldn't be seeing more stars if a horse had kicked him in the head. Standing in his office with her high-topped feet apart, her hands crammed into the front pocket of her lightweight hoodie and her curves far too visible underneath those skin-tight exercise pants or whatever the hell they were, she was the image of defiance. Of her *mother.*

She was also a seventeen-year-old girl—*his* seventeen-year-old girl—who shouldn't even be *thinking* about babies, unless it was to sit for somebody else's.

"You p-promised you wouldn't have a cow."

"You're lucky I'm not having a whole damn herd!" Johnny yelled, even as he could hear Andy's *Now, son, ain't no sense blowin' a gasket over every little thing.* Only there was nothing *little* about this; this was far, far worse than the hair. *This* was an out-and-out disaster. "And how long have you been lying to me about not havin' sex?"

"Johnny," Thea said quietly, warningly, behind him, and he thought, *Yeah, like I need to be dealing with you on top of everything else.* Because he hadn't seen her in months and she looked like hell and at this rate he wasn't gonna find out why anytime soon—

"Like I was really gonna tell you about that?" Rachel said, tears slipping, and Johnny thought, *Right. Daughter. Pregnant. Crap,* as the other half of this idiocy—looking like he wished he was dead—had the good sense to turn beet red. "Geez, Dad—get real. Jess and me, we've been together for two years. Did you think we were going to wait forever?"

"Yes."

"Sir—"

"You," Johnny said, his jabbed finger in Jesse's direction provoking a highly satisfactory flinch, "I'll deal with later. Right now this is between my daughter and me."

"Sir," Jesse said again, pale, his beefy hand landing possessively on Rachel's shoulder. "N-not to argue with you or anything, but it's my k-kid Rach's carrying. So I think that g-gives me some say in the matter."

"Fine." Johnny crossed his arms, considering handing the kid a trash can to barf into. "Then tell me how you plan on taking care of my daughter and *your kid.* You didn't even go to college, for God's sake!"

"Dad!" Rachel cried as terror flashed in the boy's dark eyes. "That's so unfair!"

"Haven't gotten that far in my thinking yet," Jess said, his Adam's apple working overtime. "Since, y'know, I just found out. But…" Sweat glowed on the kid's bald head. "But…but I know I…" His gaze dropped to Rachel's, who was looking at him with such trust and adoration Johnny felt sick. Jesse's eyes cut back to Johnny. "I'll figure something out, sir," he repeated. Limply.

Still, it took guts, standing up to somebody mad enough to rip apart the side of a barn with his bare hands, especially when you felt like you'd just gotten caught in a trash compactor…and didn't that bring back a slew of bitter memories? God knew Johnny'd been holding his breath for the past two years, praying for this thing between Jesse and his daughter to "blow over"—what his brainy daughter saw in this punk, Johnny had no idea—but he'd give him props for this much.

"Daddy." At the single, defiant word, Johnny's gaze swung back to Rachel, suspicion flaring. Her chin lifted. "I'm not unhappy about this."

While Rach had never been overtly rebellious, she was nothing if not headstrong. It had been her decision to return to Tierra Rosa for high school, wanting nothing to do with the "creepy" private school in Manhattan her mother had probably bribed half the city to get her into. A decision that didn't even make sense to Johnny, let alone Kat. What girl in her right mind would give up the good life on Manhattan's Upper East Side to come back to some podunk town in northern New Mexico? To live with her barely high-school-educated father on his barely profitable ranch?

Fix this, he heard over the sensation of somebody using a paint scraper on his insides. *Make it better, make it go away...*

Yeah. Like he'd been so successful at that nearly eighteen years ago.

"What about school? And college? You were so excited about getting into Stanford—"

"School's done in three weeks. And Stanford was Mom's idea, not mine."

News to me, Johnny thought, his eyebrows shooting up. "And where are you going to live? And do your parents know?" he lobbed at Jesse, who reddened again, before turning again to Rachel. "Does your *mother* know? God, Rach—did either of you think through any of this, what having a baby would do to your futures—"

"Of course I thought about it!" Rachel slammed back, and Johnny felt something cold and slimy snake up his spine.

His voice dropped to his boots. "Please don't tell me you got pregnant on purpose."

Blushing, his daughter glanced at her boyfriend, who looked like he'd just swallowed a slug of antifreeze, then back at Johnny. "Not exactly. I just didn't think it would happen so fast."

"Oh, Rach, no," Thea said in a low, pained voice, and Johnny's head whipped around to his ex-lover, looking strangely vulnerable in that stupid little-girl top she was wearing. A strange choice, considering her constant battle for people to take her seriously, what with her being barely the size of a gnat. Truthfully, he'd at first kinda resented that Thea and Rach had continued their relationship after the breakup, but in the long run he'd been grateful. Especially since God knew his daughter needed *some* kind of female influence in her day-to-day life—

"You didn't tell me that part," Thea said on a sigh.

"You knew?"

Thea blinked at him. "About three minutes before you did—"

"Nobody's trying to keep a secret from you, Dad," Rachel said, only to redden again when Johnny's gaze swung back to hers. "That's why I'm here now. Telling you. Because I wanted you to know. But…but we don't have all the answers. Actually, I guess we don't have any of the answers. Not yet. Except…" She slipped her hand into Jesse's. "Except we want to get married."

Johnny almost laughed. "No damn way."

"Dad!"

"You really think I'm gonna let you make *two* mistakes?"

"*Dad!* You're being totally *unfair!*"

"Fair has nothing to do with it—"

"It's *my* life," Rachel cried. "And now that I'm having a baby, you can't tell me what to do anymore! Not you, or Mom, or anybody!"

Her rubber soles slammed into the worn floorboards as she ran from the room, a thoroughly confused Jesse lumbering after her, and Johnny dropped onto a hard bench underneath one of the windows, cradling his spinning head in his hands.

"Jesse! *Jesse!*" Rachel grabbed for her boyfriend as he streaked down the graveled front path, but he shook her off and kept going. "Jess…for God's sake! What's wrong?"

"What's *wrong?*" he barked, wheeling on her when they reached the end of the path. Rachel stumbled backward, her breath catching in her chest—she'd never seen him that mad before. Ever. "Are you *insane?* You *tricked* me into getting you pregnant?"

"No!" she said, feeling her face warm. "I mean…not exactly."

"And what the hell does *not exactly* mean?" Before she could answer, he swung one pointed hand back toward the house. "You blindsided me in there, Rach! In front of your dad, who already hates me—"

"He doesn't hate you, Jess—"

"You told me you were safe, that time we ran out of condoms! So, what're you saying? That you lied to me?"

"I told you I *thought* I was safe. But…but what difference does it make? We always talked about getting married, having kids—"

"*Someday,* Rach! Not now! Not *yet!* No way am I ready to be a father!" He swallowed hard, his eyes glistening. "And for you to do this to me—"

"Me to do this to *you?* Hey, you were the one too lazy to go to the store!"

His eyes turned black as night. "I would've gone, Rach. But you said…" His head slowly moving from side to side, he lifted his hands, backing away. "I gotta get out of here. I can't talk to you right now…."

He pivoted and strode toward his bike, Rachel scrambling to catch up to him. "Jess, I'm sorry!" she said as he straddled the bike, crammed on his helmet. "I thought…I thought it'd be okay."

He glared at her. "Why the *hell* would you think that?"

For the first time, something like real fear clutched at her heart. "Oh, come on, Jess…it's not like we didn't know there was a risk! Even when we were using something! And you said you were okay with it," she said, reaching for him when he turned away, gunning the engine, "that it didn't matter because we loved each other! *Jesse!*" she screamed when he zoomed away. *"JESSEEEE!"*

Sputtering furious tears, she scooped up a dirt clod left over from the last rainstorm, the clump of dirt disintegrating when she ineffectually hurtled it at the rapidly disappearing bike.

Even as she realized she had no one to blame for this mess but her own sorry self.

Chapter Two

"Here." Amazed that her hand was steady, Thea held out a glass with an inch of whiskey in it. Slowly, Johnny lifted puzzled, troubled eyes to hers, and all she wanted was to wrap her arms around him and hold on tight. After a wordless moment, his gaze dropped back to the glass.

"What's that?"

"Something I ran across in your 'medicine cabinet.'"

He pulled a face. "Stuff's probably ten years old."

"Then it oughtta be good and ripe by now." When he looked at her again, his eyes slightly narrowed, her heart ka-thumped. "What is it?"

"You're paler than usual. You feeling okay?"

"I'm fine." She wiggled the glass, making the booze shimmer. "Drink up."

Even after he took it, though, he didn't seem in any hurry to down its contents. "Where's yours?"

"I'm not the one who needs to chill," she said, thinking, *Good save, chickie.*

"I don't need—"

"Oh, believe me, honey, you do."

Finally he knocked back the booze, then grimaced. "Damn, woman—you tryin' to kill me?"

"Think of it as puttin' you out of your misery." She sat beside him on the bench. But not too close. Normally the earthy, honest smell of a man who'd been working horses in the hot spring sun—or at least, the smell of this man—didn't bother her at all. These days, though—

"And you're here in what capacity, exactly?" Johnny asked.

"I'm thinking referee," Thea said after a brief pause, then laid her hand on his wrist. "Oh, Johnny…I'm so sorry." *More than you have any idea.*

Half smiling, Johnny leaned against the paneled wall, apparently letting the whiskey do its thing. "I guess I came down a little hard on the kids."

"You had cause."

He sighed like…well, like a man who'd just found out his teenage daughter was pregnant. "You think I should go find her? *Them?*"

"Unless you've had a change of heart in the last three minutes, I'm gonna say no."

"You can't possibly believe I should *let* her marry Jesse?"

"She's having his baby, sugar. I'm not sure you get a vote."

Johnny squinted at the empty glass in the sunlight. "Unfortunately, Rach is still gonna be pregnant when this wears off."

"I know," Thea said gently, hurting for him. Especially considering he had no idea about the other shoe she was dangling over his head.

"Damn, Thea," he said softly. "I miss you."

"You miss the sex," she said, not missing a beat. And not

particularly surprised, considering his woebegone expression when they'd broken up.

"No, I miss *you.* Okay, and the sex. I'd have to be dead not to miss the sex."

At Thea's sigh, Johnny slid a sad, hopeful grin in her direction. She sighed again. "Okay, I miss you, too."

"So the sex *was* good?"

And wasn't that just like a man, constantly looking for an ego boost? Especially when it came to bedroom matters. When her mouth tucked up at the corners, Johnny chuckled, real low in his throat, like he used to when they'd be finished and lying tangled up in her bed, and she'd stretch, all cat-in-the-cream-like, and Johnny'd get that *Again, please?* glint in his eyes…

Yeah, just like that, she thought. Or maybe that was the booze. *Please, God, let it be the booze—*

"So…?" he said, all goofy-grinnin', and she thought, *Nope, not the booze.*

"The sex wasn't *that* good."

"Oooh, honey, that's harsh."

Thea patted Johnny's knee with deliberate condescension, knowing that if she had a hope in hell of getting through what she had to tell him—whenever that turned out to be—she had to make it crystal clear there'd be no traveling down certain roads again. No matter how badly she wanted to leave her hand on that hard, muscled thigh. "What it is is over."

Johnny's pushed breath told her he knew she spoke the truth, which should've been more of a relief than it was. She'd have to work on that. Then he frowned at her.

"How'd you happen to be here, anyway? We've barely spoken in months."

"Rach called me," she said, grateful she didn't have to lie.

"She wanted you to get her back?"

Also true. "Apparently so."

Johnny faced front again. "This is my fault."

"How on earth do you figure that?"

"I should've kept a closer eye on her, should've…I don't know." He grimaced. "Something. Kat's gonna blow a fuse."

"Oh, and you think this couldn't've happened on your ex's watch? That girls don't get pregnant in New York City? Kids have sex, Johnny. Just like they've always done, if they want it bad enough. I sure as hell did. And no, that doesn't mean I'm condoning teenage sex. But reality is what it is. So no beating yourself up about this, you hear me? Why're you looking at me like that?"

"You never told me you had sex when you were a kid."

"I was sixteen, it wasn't anybody you know and it sucked." She shrugged. "My memory of it's like seeing some outfit you just gotta have, only when you get it home it doesn't look at all like you thought it would, but you can't return it because it was a final sale, so you shove it in the back of the closet and basically forget about it."

Johnny looked a little lost for a second, then recovered to say, "But this is different. Rach's my little girl—"

"You didn't let your toddler run into traffic, for heaven's sake! She knew exactly what she was getting into."

That got a frown. "She discussed this with you?"

Oh, boy. Thea could hardly tell him that Rach had glommed onto her because—according to the girl—talking to her dad was like talking to a rock. "Only in general terms. About how a gal needs to respect herself enough to not feel pressured into doing anything she doesn't want to do." She faced him again. "And that's about all anybody can do. Other than lock her up."

"It had occurred to me."

"Rach is a good kid, Johnny," she said gently. "And so is Jesse." When Johnny looked at Thea like she'd said she'd just seen one of his horses fly, she laughed. "Maybe he's not as sharp as Rach, and maybe he went a little nuts with the tattoos, but I've known him and his brothers since they were little. He's solid and steady, he doesn't drink or do drugs and he genuinely cares about your daughter."

"He's also nineteen."

"As were we all at some point. And we all lived through it," she added when Johnny turned away, snorting in disgust. "But good kids sometimes do dumb things. That's not always a reflection on their parents. Rach also wouldn't be the first girl to marry her high school sweetheart. And make it work."

Johnny leaned forward, poking his hand through his thick, hat-headed hair, the gray hairs at his temples bristlier than the rest of it. "She also wouldn't be the first person to marry young and have it completely fall apart, either," he said bitterly, and she knew what he was getting at. All too well.

With age definitely came experience. In and of itself, not a bad thing. But with experience also came caution, tagging along like an annoying younger sibling—which was okay if it kept you out of trouble, not so much if it kept you from fully embracing life.

The way Thea saw it, Johnny wasn't so much still hung up on his ex as he was just plain scared of screwing up again. As for Thea, working at making a man fall in love with her was not her thing. If she was going to put her heart on the line, was it too much to ask that she be loved back?

However, despite Johnny's and her relationship—or lack thereof—being deadlocked, she had not completely given up on the idea of true love, because without that she figured she may as well just lie down and die. So now she said, in all earnestness, "But Rach and Jesse aren't you and Kat. You said yourself, you and your ex were a disaster waiting to happen."

"And we only got married because Kat got pregnant. How's this any different?"

"Because Rach and Jess love each other," she said carefully, watching a muscle tense in his cheek when her words lanced a still-sensitive area. She knew Johnny'd pretty much been a wreck when his marriage blew up. But she'd also gathered that although Johnny'd suggested the divorce, Kat hadn't exactly kept her relief a secret. The whole shebang had done a real head trip on the man sitting beside her, making him even more sensitive about his fathering abilities than your average divorced dad.

"Johnny, listen to me—nobody could blame you for not wanting this for Rach. But if it's really what *she* wants, then you've got two choices—be there for her, or cut her loose and see if she floats."

Horrified eyes cut to hers. "I could never turn my back on my own kid! Hell, Thea—I thought you knew me better than that! But all I have to say is…" He stood and crossed to the bar, pouring himself another shot. "I do not know how people with more than one kid survive, and that's the truth. If I had to do this all over again," he said, the glass halfway to his lips, "I think I'd kill myself."

Yeah, about that, she thought, thinking this would probably be a good time to make her exit. Except, unfortunately, she'd been blessed—or cursed, more likely—with a face like a damned billboard. And despite Johnny's being saddled with that pesky Y chromosome, he'd always been remarkably adept at knowing when something was bothering her. That he hadn't today was understandable, given the circumstances. But now—bless his heart—his radar apparently kicked in, because he lowered the glass, frowning at her.

"Thea? What's going on?" he said, not two seconds before a swearing Rachel came crashing through the front door and stomped down the hall toward her room. Johnny's head jerked toward the swearing and the stomping, and Thea thought, *Hallelujah, a reprieve.*

"You go on," she said, but he'd already turned back to her, color drained from face.

"Oh, hell. Not you, too?"

After a very long moment, she nodded, and Johnny stared at her for about ten seconds with that recently Tasered look, before, strangely, erupting in laughter. Then all at once he stopped, like somebody'd flipped a switch, suddenly worried eyes raking her up and down.

"You're…okay?"

"So far, so good," she said, and he clutched the back of his neck as he looked away, muttering, and Thea said, "You should probably see to Rachel," and Johnny swiveled back around so fast she took a step backward.

"Don't even *think* about leaving," he said, then took off, leaving Thea to wonder why life never seemed to go the way you saw it in your head.

Johnny strode down the hall, thinking if he didn't have a coronary it'd be a damn miracle. The only positive thing—if you could call it that—was that each crisis kept him from fully concentrating on the other, at least enough to keep his head from exploding. Then he banged on his daughter's door, yelling, "Let me in, Rach," and she screamed back, "Forget it!" and he heard a soft *ka-boom,* anyway.

Johnny leaned a forearm on the door frame, breathing a little harder than he might have liked. Although it wasn't like he and Rach hadn't had their set-tos a time or six before, he had to admit he might've overreacted a little bit ago. So much that Thea's announcement still hadn't fully registered.

One thing at a time, buddy, he thought over the stab of utter disbelief, then knocked on his daughter's door again.

"I'm sorry I blew up at you, honey," he said, as gently as he knew how. Johnny'd never been real comfortable with the whole male-sensitivity thing, which was why it'd shocked the hell out of him when Rach'd asked to come live with him a few years back. But it was also a major reason him and Thea got along so well, because Thea wasn't the kind of woman who needed a lot of finessing—

Focus, man, focus....

"Rach? C'mon, honey...open the door. I'm not gonna yell, I promise—"

"You can't fix things this time, Daddy, okay? You're right, I screwed up, and nobody can straighten out my mess but me! So just...go away." He heard her blow her nose. "I'll be f-fine," she said in a tiny, frightened voice, and Johnny's heart split right down the middle.

"I'm not goin' anywhere until you open this door and show me you're okay."

Then, because he knew his daughter—stubborn as a mule under the best of circumstances—Johnny lowered his carcass onto the rough-hewn Mexican bench across the hall to wait. Which, as favorite activities went, ranked right up there with delivering a breech foal at 3:00 a.m. in the middle of a raging blizzard. Although at least that was doing something. At least that had a goal. Instead of sitting here with nothing to do except think. And worry. About Rach. About Thea. Oh, dear God, Thea...

Johnny curled forward, dragging his hands down his face as the guilt-stricken look on Thea's face, right before Johnny guessed her secret, registered. Damn—what was that he'd said about not wanting another kid? Not that it wasn't true: the idea of starting all over again with the feedings and the diapers and all the rest of it made his blood run cold. But he'd deal. Just like he'd done before—

He jerked when Rachel's lock clicked, her door slowly opening. Seeing her tearstained cheeks and swollen eyes, he was instantly on his feet, yanking his baby girl into his arms before she could slam the door shut again. To his immense relief, she molded herself against him, like she used to when she was tiny. When she trusted him not to go stupid on her.

"We'll get through this, baby," Johnny whispered into her tri-colored, girly-smelling hair. "If you and Jesse want to get married—"

On a wail, Rachel burrowed farther into his chest, and Johnny thought, Huh—maybe he wasn't the bad guy here. Which didn't cheer him nearly as much as he might have hoped.

He steered her back to sit on her frilly pink bedspread, at odds with the rough-log headboard and the deep purple, rock-star-postered walls, all of it at odds with the room's inhabitant, this woman-child who scared the hell out of him, the only person in the world who had his whole heart.

"Problems?" he asked, awkwardly stroking his daughter's shoulder. Raccoon eyes peered up at him.

"You heard?"

"I'm guessing."

She sighed. "Please don't gloat, okay?"

"I'm not. Swear to God," he said, when she gave him That Look. "Baby, you caught me off guard. And you had to know I wasn't gonna see this as good news. I still don't. How can I, when..." He rubbed his jaw. "It's like history repeating itself."

Rach eased away to grab a tissue from her nightstand, blow her nose. "You mean Mom and you?"

"Yeah. Look, I know you think you and Jesse are different—"

"Correction—*thought* Jess and I were different."

Johnny pushed her long, strangely colored hair over her shoulder. "What happened?"

The corners of her mouth sagging, Rachel yanked three more tissues from the box, looking almost more put out with herself than unhappy. "I guess…I didn't exactly clear things with Jesse as well as I thought. About us having a baby. Getting married. He says he's too young."

"For once, I have to agree with him. You're *both* too young." When she pulled a face, he said, "Why, Rach? With your brain, you could've done anything you wanted—"

"Geez, Dad—don't you get it? This *is* what I want! Why do you think I asked to come live with you when I turned twelve and found out I actually had a say in the matter? I *hated* New York. And I know I'm probably the only teenager who wants to stay in the sticks, but…" She shook her head. "This is *home,* Dad. Just like it is for you. I already know what my options are. And I've made my choice."

Johnny leaned forward, his hands clasped between his knees. "You realize your mother's gonna be wrecked."

Rach picked up a mangy stuffed bear she'd had since she was a baby, hugging it to her. "Okay, it's not like I don't respect Mom and what she's accomplished. But that's her life. Not mine. Sure, she's successful, and I guess she's happy…but I wouldn't be. And for a long time I felt so guilty that I didn't have this burning ambition to be…I don't know. Something *more* than myself. Then I got to know Thea, and I realized that being myself was just fine."

"Thea?"

Rachel shifted on her bed, cross-legged, her eyes bright again. "She's totally cool with who she is, you know? Says it's all about keeping things simple."

Johnny snorted. "You think parenthood is simple?"

"No, of course not. But it's real. And it's what I want. *All*

I want. What I've wanted since I was a little girl. And I'm not ashamed of that." She leaned over to thread her arms around Johnny's ribs, leaning her head against his shoulder. "And I'm going to be the best mom in the world. Even if I have to do it all by myself."

On a sigh, Johnny hugged his daughter back. "What makes you think you'll have to do this by yourself?"

Rachel snuggled closer. "You're the best," she whispered. "Seriously."

Johnny shut his eyes against the pain.

Seriously.

Okie-dokie, Thea thought after ten minutes alone in Johnny's office, this kid-waiting-to-see-the-principal thing was for the birds. Especially when the increasingly familiar school-of-piranhas sensation started up in her stomach.

A good sign, according to everything she'd read.

So she made her way to the large, no-nonsense kitchen at the other end of the house where Ozzie, Johnny's five-hundred-year-old cook, was tending a large, bubbling pot on the plain white gas range, the savory scent overriding the perpetual stain of fried onions and strong coffee.

On the plank table in the center of the kitchen lay the fixings for apple pie, a cookie sheet dotted with rounds of biscuit dough. At the end of the table sat Carlos, Johnny's manager and only a hundred years or so younger than Ozzie finishing up a piece of cake and a cup of coffee. Both men—who'd come with the ranch—lived on the property, Ozzie in a three-bedroom "cabin" a hundred yards or so from the house, Carlos in a cozy apartment above the mares' barn.

Now a pair of curious gazes shot to her, then to each other before Carlos stood and slugged back his coffee. "Miss Thea!" he said in his heavy Spanish accent, his face as wrinkled as his denim shirt. "Haven' seen you aroun' for a while. You doing okay?"

Bright smile time. "Sure am, Carlos. Thanks."

Another exchanged glance preceded the old man's nod, then his heavy-footed retreat. Feeling a certain rheumy gaze hot on her back, Thea marched across the terminally scuffed linoleum to the Nixon-era brown fridge, and yanked open the door. This was a room all about purpose, not style. No cutesy plates or dish-towel calendars or cheery clocks livened up the dull white walls; no curtains softened the sun's afternoon glare. But nobody who set foot inside the gentle black giant's kitchen left hungry, his hearty, homestyle cooking designed to fill stomachs and warm souls.

"What in the devil's name you doin' here?"

"Lookin' for something to eat. What's good?"

"You in *my* icebox and you got the nerve to ask me what's good?"

"Be still my heart—is that fried chicken?"

"Mos' likely, since that's what we had last night. I believe there's mashed potatuhs and gravy, too, if nobody pulled a locust number after I went on to bed."

Loaded down with containers of chicken, potatoes and gravy, Thea hip-slammed the fridge door shut, dumped the tubs on the scrubbed-bald laminate counter and grabbed a plate from the wood cabinet above.

"You ain't answered my question," Ozzie said as Thea piled enough food on the plate to feed twenty. "Ain't seen you since January, and suddenly here you are in my kitchen like some phantom, eatin' up all my food. You got a fugitive stashed in the barn or somethin'?"

Not in the barn, no. "I didn't eat much for lunch," she lied, shoving the mounded plate into the microwave—the only appliance less than twenty years old. Then she faced the old dude, her arms crossed over her growling stomach. In the pre–civil rights '50s, Ozzie and his wife, Delores, had moved to New Mexico from the deep south, finding sanctuary in a state that had been doing the assimilation thing for a good half century, with an employer who made sure Ozzie and Dee's four children went on to college. Far as anybody could tell, Ozzie was older than God, nearly as smart and every bit as meddling.

"And like you weren't in the hallway listening to what was going on."

Ozzie glanced up from painstakingly layering apple slices into a homemade crust, his sly grin rearranging ripples of dark fudge wrinkles. "I got the gist."

The microwave dinged; Thea pulled out her plate, chomping a huge bite off a chicken leg before even shutting the door. "You don't sound real surprised," she mumbled around the mouthful, plopping down in Carlos's abandoned seat.

Ozzie's shoulders rose in a slow-motion shrug as age-palsied hands unfolded the top crust over the filled bottom. "You get to be my age, ain't many surprises left. Young folks've been givin' in to temptation since the world began—nothin' new about that. Miss Rachel's no different'n anybody else. 'Specially since I could've told her daddy months ago she was headed in that direction."

There was no censure in his words, no judgment, Ozzie being more than content to leave that part of things to the Good Lord. But to be honest, Thea could've told Johnny the same thing. Not necessarily that Rachel would get pregnant, but every attempt to give Johnny a heads-up had been met with adamant denial, that Rachel had more sense than that, that she wasn't like the other girls.

"You hear the part about them wanting to get married?" she said, breaching her gravy dam with her fork.

Ozzie snorted out a breath. "You missed the fight, then?"

"Fight?"

"Right out there at the end of the drive. I couldn't hear that good, but I gather our boy Jesse ain't exactly *down,* as my grandkids would say, with his impending fatherhood. If you recall, it wasn't Jesse pushing for this marriage. Judging from Miss Rachel's dramatic entrance a few minutes ago, I'm guessing things ain't exactly goin' her way."

"Oh, hell."

"You might say."

Beginning to wonder if she was carrying a pack of wolf cubs, Thea attacked a chicken thigh, muttering, "What a mess," around the bite.

Carefully crimping the crust edges, Ozzie said, "And how far along are *you?*"

Thea lowered the mangled chicken to her plate and licked her fingers. "Heard that part, too, didja?"

"Actually, no, I left before that. But you watch a woman in the family way four times, you get to know the signs pretty good. Like you eatin' like you never seen food before. And don't look now, but you got you some *curves.* They look good on you, too."

"And here I thought I was doing such a good job of hiding it."

"Not from anybody who knows what they're lookin' at. But then, I s'pose our Johnny's better at tellin' when a mare's carrying than a woman."

"He was also a little preoccupied."

"I'll just bet he was. Must be somethin', getting two shocks like that in one day." His gaze sidled over to hers, then slid away. "Never did understand why the two of you broke it off."

"Because it was…a fling, Ozzie. That giving-in-to-temptation thing isn't only the province of the young," she said at Ozzie's eyebrow lift. "It'd run its course, that's all."

"Uh-huh," Ozzie said in a way that made Thea want to clobber him with one of his own skillets. "So you came out here to tell Johnny he was gonna be a daddy again," he said, carting the pie to the stove, the oven door squawking when he opened it, "and Miss Rachel stole your thunder."

"Yep, that's about the size of it." On a groan, Thea pushed away her empty plate to plunk her elbows on the table and cradle her head in her hands. "I feel so bad for Johnny, Oz. Things were gonna be tough enough without that wrinkle."

The oven door slammed shut, Ozzie lifted the pot lid and stirred. "But you want this baby?"

She sighed. "You have no idea how much I want this baby. It's all the rest of it I could do without."

"Then you of all people should know," he said, the lid rattling back in place before he turned to her, "that life don't come in permanent press. And why should you feel bad for Johnny? It's not like you got in this condition by yourself."

"Yeah, well, it wasn't like we were *trying* to make this baby, either." At Ozzie's raised eyebrow, she mumbled, "You know what I mean."

"Oh, I know what you mean, all right," he said, chuckling softly. "I also know if anybody can make lemonade outta lemons, it's Johnny. Sometimes, the things in life that take us most by surprise turn out to be the biggest blessings. So don't you go thinking this baby—or the one Miss Rachel's carryin', neither—is a mistake. A surprise, maybe, but no *child's* a mistake."

What Thea was thinking was that she'd dearly love to know what *God* was thinking. Why He'd chosen now to work the miracle thing. And why oh *why* He'd chosen Johnny as the means to this particular end—

"You see anybody yet?" Ozzie asked. "About the baby?"

Yeah, and wasn't that gonna bring a certain somebody's wrath down around her head?

"Oh. Um, no, not yet—"

"My Naomi moved back a couple months ago, set up a family practice just north of town."

"Really? Mama took me to see her a few times, when I was a kid. She's good folks."

Ozzie dug into his shirt pocket and handed Thea a card, still obviously proud as a peacock that his daughter was a *doctor.* "No, go on, I can get more."

Thea reluctantly took the card, another shiver of apprehension rolling through her as Ozzie trundled over to a footed cake tray. Not because of Naomi Wilson, though—from what Thea remembered, a nicer, kinder human being didn't exist. Because of everything going to see her implied. Still, she'd already put it off longer than she probably should have.

"It's yesterday's," Ozzie said, lifting the translucent cover to reveal a four-layer chocolate cake, "but still fresh. You want a slice while you wait?"

"Maybe you should make that to go," Johnny said from the doorway, making Thea jump. Then frown.

"First you tell me to stay put, now you're throwing me out?"

His smile looked like it took a supreme effort. "Not hardly. But we need to talk, and I've got work to do. May as well put my multitasking skills to good use."

"Here." Ozzie handed her a huge slab of cake in a plastic storage tub, along with a napkin and a fork. "You stayin' for supper? We got plenty."

Thea looked at Johnny, who wore the expression of a man hoping to wake up and discover he'd just had a bad dream.

"I'll let you know," she said, then followed Johnny outside, thinking anytime God felt like cluing her in to His purpose would be fine with her.

Chapter Three

"I thought we were supposed to be talking," Thea tossed to Johnny as she trotted along behind him, shoveling in cake as fast as she could get fork to mouth and wondering, between the trotting, the shoveling and the distraction that was Johnny's backside, how she managed not to stab herself. He might not be some movie-star cowboy with long legs and a graceful gait, but what his Creator had given him was definitely something to behold. Especially when you added anger and—she suspected—extreme frustration to the mix.

"Working up to it," he said, then suddenly turned, a frown the size of the Grand Canyon etched between his brows. "You got any idea what it feels like inside my head right now? Any idea at all? Between my daughter pulling a fast one on her boyfriend, and my ex-girlfriend—"

"Lover," Thea put in, not that he noticed.

"—turning up pregnant..." Angry, troubled eyes dropped

to hers. "Just when it seems like things couldn't get any worse, they do."

Yeah, that's about the reaction she figured on. In some perverted way, it was a relief. Nowhere to go from here but up. "Is Rach okay? Ozzie said the kids had a fight."

Heaving a breath, Johnny resumed walking. At a normal pace, bless him. "Turns out Rach and Jess aren't exactly on the same page."

"Oh, no…poor Rach," Thea said, caught up. In more ways than one. She forked in another bite of cake, moist and chocolaty and hopefully with healing powers beyond reason. "I thought you didn't want them to get married?"

"Frankly, I don't know what to think," Johnny grumbled. "Or do. Don't know what makes me want to retch more—Rach bein' a teenage pregnancy statistic or her marrying Jesse. Girl's always been muleheaded, I suppose because of what happened between her mother and me, but this beats all. Half of me's still so mad I can't think straight, but the other half hurts like hell for her. Why are you lookin' at me like that?"

"Just wondering if you're mad at me, too."

He almost smiled, if grimly. "I'm mad, period. About all of it. But especially with myself, for lettin' things get out of hand." *Oh, for pity's sake,* she thought, only to jerk when Johnny said, "Did you know Rach apparently sees you as some sort of role model?"

"Ex*cuse* me?"

"Not about getting pregnant," he said, and she thought, *Well, that's something, at least.* "About being content with what she's got, right here."

"She might be confusing contentment with bein' realistic, but whatever. In any case, I wasn't waging some sort of Love the Town You're In campaign, either. And I certainly never said anything to discourage her from going to college. I swear," she added when he cast a doubtful look in her direction as they reached the barn, Thea hanging back as Johnny went on ahead to a stall about halfway down. A half dozen or so barn cats lazily regarded her from where they lay in scraps of soft, dusty sunlight or desultorily prowling the dirt floor; one pushy tortoiseshell offered a halfhearted meow in welcome.

"What this place needs," she said, "is a dog. Or two."

"The cats might take issue with you on that," Johnny said, unlatching the stall door. Crazy as he was about all things equine, Johnny'd never been big on dogs. Something about his mother's needy, yippy little Chihuahuas having put him off dogs forever, she remembered, clamping a hand over her nose. Not that Johnny didn't keep his barns regularly mucked out, but horses weren't exactly potty trained. Nor did they take many bubble baths—

"Hey, sweetheart," Johnny was crooning to a gorgeous white-and-brown-spotted mare with a Jean Harlow blond mane, and everything inside Thea melted at the change come over him, watching him ease into the world he'd called "home" for more than twenty years. He slipped a halter over the horse's head, whispering to her as he carefully began to stroke her bulging side.

"How's the girl today?" he murmured, his voice stripped of the frustration that had choked it just minutes before, his grip on the mare's halter firm as she restlessly shifted at his touch, her ears flicking back and forth. "Whoa, sweetheart," he said, expertly dodging a keep-your-mitts-to-yourself hoof—a move, Thea thought ruefully, she'd used more than once herself. Although not, it should be noted, on Johnny. "No need to get excited, I'm just gonna check and see how your baby's doin', okay?"

Damn hormones, Thea thought as unexpected tears crowded the corners of her eyes. It'd been a long, long time since she'd indulged herself with wanting what wasn't hers to have. With not being okay with the moment. But watching Johnny go all sweet and tender with that horse—

Enough of this. "What's her name?"

"Bella. Short for Isabella." Johnny gave Thea a bemused look. Probably because she was standing so far away. Because, smells aside, horses were big. And she wasn't.

"It's okay, she won't hurt you," Johnny said, in the manner of someone talking to a child scared of a puppy.

"A girl can't be too careful," Thea said, thinking it was just as well things hadn't worked out between them, what with her being afraid of horses and all. "And, honey, if I was that pregnant—" because from here the poor animal looked like she was carrying a tractor "—I wouldn't want some stranger invading my personal space, either. Heck, she doesn't look all too thrilled with you poking at her, and she knows you."

"Not that well, actually. She's not mine, I'm just boarding her until she foals."

Thea frowned. "Isn't May kinda late for foaling?"

Johnny gave her a funny look, like he was surprised she'd stored up that bit of information. Then, as his hand slipped underneath the mare's belly, he grunted out, "Seems to be the season for surprise pregnancies."

"Har, har."

Sparing Thea a tight grin, Johnny straightened up again to wipe his hand on an old rag lying nearby. "Neighboring stallion jumped the fence and had his way with her."

From twenty feet away, Thea met the animal's soulful gaze. "And you didn't exactly say 'no,' did you?"

At Bella's emphatic head shake, Johnny smirked. "Her owners are away all summer," he said, taking off the halter, "so I'm playing nursemaid until they return. Sorry, girl," he said with a firm pat to her neck, "looks like another couple of days yet."

Bella tossed her magnificent head, looking put out as all hell. Chuckling, Johnny gave the sturdy, sleek neck a final pat before he let himself out of the stall, his expression sobering as he approached Thea. "So," he said, his voice as cautious as it had been with the horse, "everything check out okay with *your* baby?"

"Actually," Thea said, briefly tempted to lie, "I haven't seen anyone yet."

Johnny's eyebrows flew up. "Are you *nuts?* For God's sake, Thea, I would've thought, especially with your history—"

"And every one of those miscarriages happened *after* I went to the doctor. Each time, they told me I didn't miscarry because of anything I'd done, that it was something wrong with the baby, not me. That there was nothing anybody could've done to save 'em. Why would this time be any different? And don't look at me like that. You lose three babies, you learn not to get your hopes up."

"But—"

"But what?" she said wearily. "You know what the doctors did—all three of 'em? Gave me vitamins, a 'what to eat while you're pregnant' pamphlet, told me I should probably avoid sex for the first trimester and to come back in a month. Oh, and if I started to bleed? To let them know."

"That's it?"

"Yeah." Tears burned her eyes. "*Now* do you get it?"

Johnny gave her one of those helpless, pissed looks men get when things get too emotional, then walked past her and on outside. Sighing mightily, Thea followed, to what she knew was one of his favorite places on the ranch—the edge of a pasture with a mind-blowing view of the Sangre de Cristo mountains to the south, close to a cottonwood-shaded pond. Nearby, several horses peacefully grazed or simply chilled, tails swishing and muscles rippling underneath sleek, sun-soaked backs.

"Can you imagine what your mother would have thought,"

Thea quietly asked when Johnny propped one wrist on the wire fence, "if she'd lived to see you with all this?"

Johnny's dark gaze darted to hers before he jerked his head around again. "You mind giving me a moment, here?"

"Not at all, take your time," she said, lowering herself to the ground a few feet away, finishing off her cake while she waited.

Because she knew better than to rush him. Shortly after she'd moved back to Tierra Rosa and long before they'd gotten cozy—both of them recently divorced and more in need of somebody to simply talk to than anything—Johnny'd told her about his hothead teenage years when he'd been angry and defensive about pretty much everything, years Johnny saw as a remarkably unproductive period in his life that had nearly cost him everything, especially his self-respect. As a result, she knew he was hugely uncomfortable with any emotion that made him feel as out of control as he'd felt then, although he'd never admitted this in so many words.

Thea's own feelings on the subject were mixed, at best. Her initial reaction had been to chalk the whole thing up to yet another male excuse for keeping his distance…until she realized, on this point at least, they were far more alike than not. Yeah, life had toughened both of them up pretty good, taught them that the best defense against pain was to never leave yourself vulnerable to begin with. Strong emotion—especially anger, especially *love*—was scary as all hell.

And boy, could she relate to that. Not that she had issues with ripping someone a new one if the situation warranted it, but the leaving yourself open thing? Sing it, sister. For too many years, she watched her mother hold together her own marriage through sheer willpower, a marriage that by the time Thea reached puberty she'd figured out wasn't worth the price of the license. Only then what did she do but marry a man who controlled practically her every move in the name of "taking care" of her, while handily *taking care* of his own needs in beds other than the one he shared with his wife.

Thea smashed the back of her fork into what was left of the cake, pretending it was a certain someone's you-know-whats.

Disgusted—because how could she eat it now?—Thea set the pulverized mess aside, then linked her arms around her bent knees, her thighs pushing against her rapidly expanding middle.

Another tremor shuddered through her, the kind that made her avoid baby departments or baby name books that had her petrified she'd see blood every time she went to the bathroom. That had kept her from telling Johnny she was pregnant until now.

That stopped her from looking any further ahead than one day at a time.

Eyes shut, Thea lifted her fingers to press them against her temples, breathing deeply. Refusing to give in to the tears. To self-pity. Sometimes she half believed God had been looking out for her, not letting her have those babies she so desperately wanted, babies that would have—she finally realized—trapped her in a situation that would have eventually killed her spirit altogether. Of course, that didn't account for all the women in equally bad—if not a whole lot worse—situations who popped out babies like they were going out of style, so she knew her reasoning was a bit shaky.

So that's why, as strong as her feelings for Johnny might have been, for sure she wasn't dumb enough to let those feelings overpower her, or to cede that kind of control, ever again, to another human being.

Not even the father of the child she didn't yet dare believe she would have.

Still leaning against the fence, Johnny watched Thea, her eyes tightly shut, her arms now wrapped around her middle. He was half convinced he could smell her fear.

What he could catch over his own, that is.

He looked back over the pasture, thinking how scary this must be for her. Yeah, the others had all been early miscarriages, but still. She'd wanted those babies, wanted them bad, and even when she'd told him—a good five years after the last one—he could tell she still mourned them. Not obsessively, not to the point where it interfered with her life, but the grief was still there.

At the time, Johnny'd felt bad for her, sure, but only in a distant sort of way—partly because they weren't his babies and he couldn't entirely relate, partly because Thea made it clear his pity was unwelcome. He'd certainly understood that part—moving on was next to impossible with people feeling sorry for you.

Except now he could relate. Now the fear was his, too. For her, for him, for—much to his shock—the baby he hadn't even known about an hour ago.

None of which he dared tell her.

Hadn't been a damn thing he could say, when she'd broken things off between them. Because she'd been right: theirs had been a relationship headed nowhere fast. Johnny'd been crazy in love once before, had let himself go where he knew he had no business being, and it had damn near killed him, left him feeling powerless. Lost. And he'd hated it. Hated even more the devastation left in its wake when it was over. Love was just too damn unpredictable. Slippery.

All of which Thea not only knew before they got involved, but—and here was the kicker—*agreed with.* Wholeheartedly. Even so, women…they might talk the talk about being okay with a casual affair, but in practice it almost never worked out that way. But did that stop him? No.

And what had suffered most? Their friendship, that's what. Before they'd gone and gotten naked with each other, they'd had an honest-to-God, no-bull relationship, the kind that was rare enough between men, let alone between a man and a woman. She'd made him forget. Feel…almost complete. But now…

Now they had to tiptoe around each other, picking and choosing their words.

Stupid.

"You ready to talk yet?" she said softly, and his eyes dropped to her belly, barely curved underneath the loose top, and something hot and sharp raced through him. But something tender, too. The old protectiveness thing kicking in, he supposed. Because taking care of things, of people, was what he did. Had done, for as long as he could remember. Overcompensation?

Maybe.

He turned away. "You're the one who decided not to tell me for…how long was it again?"

"Don't," she said. Simply. Tiredly.

"So Rachel had nothing to do with your coming out here, did she?"

"No. I didn't know about Rach until after I got here. And once I did…" He heard a stone or something thud in the dirt. "I almost didn't tell you."

"You didn't. I guessed."

"Yeah, but I was working up to it."

"What made you change your mind?"

"The thought of having to work up to it all over again."

Johnny blew a half laugh through his nose, thinking that nobody made him laugh—as often and as inappropriately—as this woman. That even under these circumstances he felt better being with her than not. "I still don't get why you didn't tell me sooner."

"Maybe because I needed to come to terms with things before I dragged you into it, too. You're not the one tossing your cookies every five minutes—"

"Excuse me? *Drag* me into it?"

"Okay, bad choice of words. Since I've got no intention of dragging you into anything. Especially since…" She poked one hand through her short hair, the ends just grazing her jawline. "There didn't seem to be much point before now. That's all."

"And maybe I could've helped."

"How?" she said, her expression incredulous.

"Maybe by just being there, okay? So you didn't have to go through all that worrying alone." When she averted her gaze, he said, "Just because we're not together anymore doesn't mean I've written off what we had. Before, I mean," he added when her eyes slanted back up to his. Eyes that, despite the fierce glint of independence and self-preservation, glittered with barely disguised disappointment. *Par for the course,* he thought, looking away. Stupidly pouring salt in the wound, he said, "It's not like I don't care about you, Thea. I'd like to think we're still friends. And I do miss you—"

A sudden thought chilled him.

"If…if you'd lost the baby, would you have even told me?"

Another stone or something hit the ground. "I don't know," she said, then met his gaze again. "Probably. Eventually. Hell," she said on a breath, "I'm only telling you now because you've got a right to know. Since you've made your feelings more than clear about havin' another kid. And now with Rach being pregnant, too—"

"And last time I checked I was perfectly capable of handling more than one crisis at a time. What do you think I'm gonna do? Turn my back on you? On my own kid?"

"A kid you don't want."

"Dammit, Thea—I can roll with the punches, okay?"

"But you're not happy about it."

"I just found out I'm gonna be a father again and a grandfather on the same day. I feel like I've just been bucked off a horse and landed on my head. Happy's not exactly what I'm feeling right now, no. But you can count on me to do whatever needs doing. Which you damn well know."

She looked away, all set mouth and stubborn chin, and Johnny blew out a breath, even as she said, "I don't want you to feel obligated."

"I can think of a lot worse things to be," he said, harsh enough to bring her head back up, her hand shielding her eyes. "Maybe this isn't exactly a Hallmark moment, but this child—and you—never have to worry about me holding up my end of the bargain. And that's a damn sight more than a lot of kids, and their mothers, ever have."

After a long moment, Thea pushed out a soft, "Well, okay. Thank you."

Johnny nodded, his gaze veering once more, his voice softening. "I'm sorry you've been sick. Kat was, too, with Rach." He looked down at her again. "Seems unfair."

Thea shrugged. "Could've been worse, I guess. I only missed work a couple of mornings." She paused, then said flatly, "It's a good sign, actually."

"You weren't sick…before?"

"Never got far enough along to *get* sick."

"No more waitressing, though. That's out."

She burst out laughing. "Says you and whose army? I feel fine now. Mostly. And you know I'd go nuts if I couldn't check in on the local gossip every morning."

"If it's the money—"

"I've got a little nest egg put aside. I'm actually okay on that score. But all those other times, the instant I thought I might be pregnant I just…stopped living. This time I didn't even fully realize I was pregnant until I was nearly three months gone—didn't even think about the possibility, frankly—so I just went about my normal life. And maybe that was the key—what I didn't know didn't have any power to hurt me. So that's what I intend to keep doing. Live my normal life. And my normal life includes waiting tables, for as long as I can."

He smirked. "You must be the only woman on earth who actually likes waitin' on people. And what if the doctor tells you to quit?"

She got to her feet, dusting off her bottom. "Then I'll take it under advisement," she said, bending down to pick up the plastic container and fork.

"And in the meantime you'd put this baby in danger?"

Her eyes flashed. "Three times, I treated myself like I was made of spun glass. Three times, I've lost my baby. This time I've been going about my business just like always and amazingly I'm still pregnant. So if it's all the same to you, I'll go with what's working, okay? Although if it makes you feel any better I'll go ahead and cancel the skydiving lessons," she said, and Johnny thought, *Hell, we can't even* fight *like normal people.*

Even so, he said, "What about that…that stuff you make? Is all that paint and varnish and what-have-you okay to breathe?"

Thea's brows lifted, her fire of moments before dissolving into a chuckle. Woman never had been the least bit ashamed about peddling her tacky-as-hell, brightly painted wooden fetish bears and jackrabbits and coyotes with bandannas around their necks, for God's sake, to unsuspecting tourists at flea markets or out of the back of her Jeep out on the highway on her days off.

"It's all nontoxic, if that's what's worrying you. And you know what? Maybe I'm no Georgia O'Keefe, but my stuff makes people happy, it makes *me* happy—"

"And where are you going to live? After the baby's born?"

Thea's smile faltered before she crossed her arms, the container tucked safely against the slight bulge. "In my house. Where else?"

"It's not a house, Thea. It's a convenience store."

"*Used* to be a convenience store. Now it's my house," she said with a warning edge to her voice. "A house, as I recall, you had no problem getting naked with me in."

"That was different," Johnny said, annoyed. Aroused. Why'd she have to go and provoke all those memories? "It's not…safe," he growled, mostly at the memories. It had been a long time for both of them, once they finally got around to it. And inhibition had not been an issue—

"Honey, a bomb shelter couldn't be safer," she was saying. "And for sure nobody's gonna break in with the dogs."

Right. The dogs. Five, at last count. None of 'em worth their weight in dog food, a couple of 'em so ugly nobody else'd want 'em, but she'd probably strangle with her bare hands anybody dumb enough to say so.

"Thea. Your front yard is a parking lot. With a dead gas pump in it."

"Better than an old toilet. Or a plastic flamingo. And you can stop shaking your head right now, Johnny Griego. Home's what you make of it. It's where you find peace, where you feel like you belong. What anybody else thinks is immaterial. And exactly where are you going with this?"

Somewhere he never in his wildest dreams imagined he'd be heading again. "You can't raise our child in a convenience store. You can't raise our child *alone.*"

"There you go again, telling me what I can't do. I can, and I will. And anyway, if I don't live there, then where? There's plenty of room for my crafts, and the dogs…. I can't give up my dogs. I *won't* give up the dogs—"

"Marry me," Johnny said, even as everything inside him

screamed *What the hell?* "I've got plenty of room for…for all of it, the baby and the dogs and the coyotes—"

"*Marry* you?" Thea screeched, her eyes going as big as the wheels on her Jeep. "Have you lost your *mind?*" Then she spun around and took off, dust flying in her wake.

"Where the hell do you think you're going?"

"Back home! And don't you dare follow me!"

He caught up to her at her car. "Think about the baby!"

She wheeled on him, mouth ajar. "Think about the baby? *Think about the baby?* What the hell—" she smacked his arm "—do you think I've been doing 24/7 for the last two months? Make sure this gets back to Ozzie," she said, shoving the container into his chest.

She yanked open the Jeep's door and scrambled up into the driver's seat; Johnny grabbed the door so she couldn't close it. "Thea, listen to me—"

"For heaven's sake, Johnny," she said, tears blooming in her eyes, making him feel crappier than he already did, "you no more want to marry me than you want to wrestle rattlesnakes! And let me go, dammit!"

"You are *not* raising this kid on your own! So we're getting married, and that's all there is to it."

"Yeah, like that worked so well for you before."

She couldn't have hit her mark any more accurately if she'd tried. And on some level, he knew she was right, that he probably was making the same mistake he'd made eighteen years ago. But what other solution was there?

"It didn't work before," he said through a tight jaw, "because things were all lopsided between Kat and me."

She just looked at him.

"Dammit, Thea," Johnny said, feeling like somebody was ripping his stomach apart, "we weren't supposed to get emotionally involved, that's what we agreed on."

"Yeah, well, I wasn't supposed to get pregnant, either."

At his start, she sighed. "Johnny…I don't need to be taken care of. Or protected. And there's nothing…" He saw her swallow. "There's nothing you can do to make sure this pregnancy sticks. I'm not gonna do anything stupid, I promise. And that includes marrying you just because I'm pregnant."

Then she put the Jeep in gear and gunned the engine, that warning look sparking again in her eyes. His hand firmly clamped on the door, he gave her one right back.

"At least promise me you'll make an appointment to see somebody. Like, yesterday."

Her mouth twisted. "As a matter of fact, Ozzie gave me his daughter's card." From underneath her lashes, her gaze cut to his. "Good enough?"

"For now," he said, finally pushing shut her door and stepping away, choking slightly in the twin plumes of dust as she sped off.

"She's scared," Ozzie said mildly when Johnny walked into the kitchen with the abandoned container. His glower provoked a shrug. "Window's open. Your voices carried."

Johnny blew out a breath. "She's had three miscarriages. So, yeah, she's scared."

"*Three?* I didn't know that. But that's not what I'm talking about. I'm talking about, she's scared on account of she don't want to get her heart broken again. Give me that thing," he said, grabbing the plastic container out of Johnny's hand. "Oh, for pity's sake…" Mumbling, Ozzie stomped over to the back door and out onto the porch to bang the container against the porch railing. "I don't suppose you noticed the ants?" came back through the door, followed by, "What on earth were you thinking, boy?"

Not about ants, that was for damn sure.

Chapter Four

For an hour or two every Wednesday afternoon, the back booth at Ortega's was a refuge of sorts for the three women currently gorging on deep-fried sopapillas and crunchy, cinnamon-sugar-dusted churros, their own chatter drowning out the raucous laughter of two young boys chasing a border collie named Annabelle—or she, them, it was hard to tell—up and down the empty restaurant. The pretty, dark-haired mother of two whose husband was on his third tour of duty in Iraq was a Tierra Rosa native like Thea; the tall, thin, very pregnant blonde had only been a resident since Thanksgiving; and then there was Thea, who'd come home after several years in Oklahoma—and a marriage that redefined *disastrous*—to lick her wounds.

It had been Winnie—the blonde, now married to the handsome, curmudgeonly, Irish artist who lived in the glass-and-wood mountain house a little ways out of town—who'd brought the three together. Winnie, who'd zeroed in on the problem between Johnny and Thea the first time she'd come into Ortega's last fall. Winnie, who now held Thea's hand as she 'fessed up about her pregnancy.

Winnie, who—as Thea figured she would—grinned right into Thea's eyes and said, in a West Texas accent not a lot different from the one Thea'd inherited from her mama, "Hot *damn,* girl! You're gonna have a baby!"

On the other hand, Tess Montoya—a big-haired brunette with Plexiglas nails, a still-newish real estate license and a seven-month-old baby girl at her breast—confined her reaction to a slightly stunned, "Oh my God."

Thea looked from one to the other. "You mean, you couldn't tell?"

The two women exchanged a glance. Then Winnie shrugged and grinned, the ends of her straight hair feathering over her shoulders. "To be honest…we were both trying to figure out how to bring up the subject—"

"—but *you* figure out a delicate way to ask someone why she's suddenly wearing baggy clothes," Tess put in.

Thea glanced down at her top. "It's hideous, isn't it?"

"Hideous, hell," Tess said. "I should look so hot in something designed for a twelve-year-old—"

"Omigosh," Winnie said as Thea squinted at the brunette, who was grinning back at her, "we're going to give birth two months apart."

At Thea's flinch, Tess said softly, "One day at a time," pulling closed her open shirt as she sat her baby daughter up to thump out a grinning, toothless belch, and Thea's eyes stung even as she smiled at the little chunker contentedly drooling around her chubby little fist. Despite her expanding belly, Itty-Bit was still more possibility than reality, an impersonal hope she didn't dare believe in just yet. Winnie squeezed Thea's hand harder.

"It's going to be fine, honey, I just know it. *All* of it," Winnie said. With heartfelt meaning.

Blinking to clear her tears, Thea laughed. "Okay, don't go expecting a happy ending between Johnny and me like what happened with you and Aidan. I've told him about the baby, and we'll deal, but anything more than that…uh-uh."

From across the table, Tess's deep brown eyes flashed, indignant. "The bastard didn't ask you to marry him?"

"Oh, he did. I said no." Thea tore off the corner of her sopapilla and drizzled honey into the warm pastry's soft, flaky cavity. "And before y'all get on my case," she said, pinching off a piece and popping it into her mouth, then licking her sticky fingers, "he's going to have enough to deal with without adding a pregnant ex into the mix." At the pair of frowns across from her, she leaned forward and whispered, "Don't you dare breathe a word of this to anyone—not even Aidan," she added with a warning glance at Winnie, who rolled her eyes, "but Rachel's pregnant, too."

"Holy crap," Tess said, while Winnie's jaw fell to her lap.

"Oh God, no. Is she—"

"Mama?" called out the tall, towheaded boy who looked exactly like Winnie. "C'n Miguel and me go outside?"

"Miguel and I. And yes, Robbie, but stay close." Her eyes shiny, Winnie turned back to Thea. "Is she gonna keep it?"

Nine years, Thea knew, Winnie had wrestled with the emotional fallout from her grandmother's basically forcing her to give up her baby son for adoption. To Aidan, as it happened, and his first wife, dead more than a year before Winnie's sudden decision to find out how Robbie was doing. That Winnie's story had an unexpectedly happy ending didn't diminish the leftover pain in her eyes one whit.

"Keep it? Are you kidding, she's absolutely thrilled. Her father, on the other hand…well, you can imagine what he's going through. Dealing with a sham marriage on top of it…" Thea shook her head. "I couldn't do that to him. Or to myself, for that matter," she said before Winnie could put in her two cents. "Not again."

A second later, Baby Julia broke into a full-out wail that signaled the end of the party, so Tess gathered her children—plus Robbie—gave Thea a big, perfumey hug, told her to call if she needed anything and left. Winnie, however—once she'd extricated herself and her basketball belly from the booth—lagged behind. Of course. Long-ingrained habit propelled Thea up to grab a tray from the serving station and begin clearing the table.

"Don't start, Win."

"Oooh, a little tetchy, are we? In any case, I was just wondering who your doctor was. Because if you don't have one, Naomi Wilson's terrific—"

"You can stop the sales pitch, I already know her. From when she was here before, when I was still a kid. My first appointment's tomorrow."

"Oh. Well. Good, then." Winnie reached over to briefly stroke Thea's arm, then folded her own over the basketball, and Thea thought, *Oh Lord…here it comes.*

"In case you forgot," Winnie said, "I was there. Or rather, here. Sitting right over at that table," she said, nodding toward the window table where Thea had waited on Winnie and Aidan, way back in October, "when I saw you and Johnny together for the first time. You never said what went down that day, but you weren't exactly all sunshine and roses when he left. Aidan said it was because of Johnny's problem with commitment. Because of his ex-wife and all."

Thinking, *And why is it I live here again?,* Thea dumped the dirty dishes into their respective bins, then turned back to her friend. "So much for not starting."

"So I lied," Winnie said as the border collie came trotting over to share the love. Unable to bear the knowing look in her friend's eyes, Thea bent down to oblige the wriggling mass of black and white fur.

"It...goes deeper than that."

"Doesn't it always?" Winnie said on a sigh, then added, "Look, I just want to make sure you're being honest with yourself. You don't want to marry the man, that's up to you—"

"Yes, it is, Winnie," Thea said, straightening to look her friend in the eye despite the fine trembling threatening to take over her body.

Instead of taking offense, Winnie gave Thea a hug. "Then I'll say no more," she whispered, letting go to grab her purse. "Hey...I'm seeing Naomi tomorrow, too. In the morning. Maybe we'll run into each other?"

"Maybe so," Thea said with a smile she most definitely did not feel.

Shortly afterward, the table cleaned and goodbyes to Evangelista and the kitchen staff dispensed, Thea climbed into her Jeep and let out a weary sigh. The good news was, she had the rest of the day to herself, in the weird little home she loved beyond all reason—in no small part because it wasn't some ticky-tacky apartment like the ones she'd lived in all her life—with the herd of mutts she loved even more. The bad news, of course, was that so much time alone provided way too much opportunity to totally freak herself out about her doctor's appointment the next day.

However, when she pulled up in front of the old Circle K, there was Rachel, leaning up against the front bumper of her little blue Toyota truck, the breeze blowing her schizoid hair across her very grumpy expression, and Thea thought, *So much for that.*

* * *

Rachel pushed herself upright, feeling like bugs were crawling around inside her stomach. "Hey, honey," Thea called over as she got out of the truck, shielding her eyes from the wicked-bright sun. From behind Thea's house, her mutts started barking like crazy. "Aren't you supposed to be at work?"

"Um…I don't have to be there until four." Rachel shifted, hugging herself. "You mind if I hang out here for a few minutes?"

"Things a little tense at your house, are they?"

"You have no idea."

"Uh, actually, I do," Thea said, but with an edge to her voice that Rachel did not find reassuring. Especially when Thea walked back out to the road to get her mail without answering her question.

Rachel chewed on her bottom lip, undecided. Wishing everything hadn't gotten so screwed up. She still wasn't sorry about the baby—God, no—but she hated how out of whack everything felt.

Thea slammed shut the mailbox, then stood there, sorting through her mail. Obviously avoiding Rachel.

She sucked in a deep breath, trying to loosen the tight feeling in her chest. What few girlfriends she'd made since coming back home had more or less fallen by the wayside once she and Jesse got together, partly because there wasn't time for school and work and Jesse *and* them, and partly because—Rachel was guessing—it pissed them off that she didn't like to talk about the relationship. Like it was their right or something to be kept in the loop about every detail of her private life.

So, basically, she got a rep for being stuck-up, the chick from New York who thought she was too good for the locals. Screw 'em, she'd thought, once she'd gotten over the worst of the sting. She had Jesse, she had Dad…and she had Thea.

Who was—or at least had been, a thought that got the bugs going again—a far better friend than any of those skanks could even *dream* of being.

So the idea of losing the only person she could really talk to, aside from Jesse—the only person she could talk to *about* Jesse—scared her to death. She'd already felt like the rug'd been pulled out from under her when Dad and Thea broke up—especially since she still couldn't figure out why—and now it was pretty obvious Thea wasn't any too happy about Rachel being pregnant.

But then, Rachel was a little pissed, too, that Thea hadn't told her *she* was pregnant.

And God, was the atmosphere tense or what? Cramming her fingers into the back pockets of her jeans, Rachel turned to look at the seriously insane garden scene Thea'd painted over the blah stucco, all these huge, crazy flowers in bright colors. When she heard Thea coming up behind her, she said, "That is so cool."

There was a pause. "You don't think it's a little…much?"

Rachel twisted back, still unable to tell where things stood between them. "Are you kidding?" She faced the murals again, wishing her heart would stop beating so hard. "It's freaking fantastic."

After a moment, something bumped her arm. A bunch of glossy catalogs, actually. "Come on. We can trash the Victoria's Secret models over banana smoothies."

"Cool," Rachel said, feeling only slightly relieved as she followed Thea through pots and planters and things choked with deep purple and egg-yolk-yellow pansies, their funny faces nodding at her in the cool spring breeze. But as Thea unlocked her front door, she smirked over her shoulder at the old gas pump.

"You know what that thing needs? A giant, crocheted cozy. I should get my mother on it."

God knows that wouldn't be any more bizarre than the rest of the place, Rachel thought as they went inside. Sure, it was roomy enough, but not only were there no interior walls, the entire front was basically one giant window. Still, between crayon-box-colored funky furnishings and dramatic swags of bright, airy fabrics over the windows, it was…fun.

Thea jerked open the stubborn back door and a river of dogs streamed inside, each one more excited to see her and Rachel than the next. She plopped down on one of the thick, heavily patterned rugs on the tiled floor to mess with Franny, a Blue Heeler cross who was, like, the sweetest dog, ever, and asked, "Are you mad at me?"

From the bedroom corner where Thea'd gone to exchange her gross waitressing shoes for a pair of cheapo flip-flops, she glanced at Rachel. "No," Thea said, passing tables and shelves filled with all her paints and stuff to get to her "kitchen," dogs waddling and panting after her. "I'm not mad at you."

"Then has your phone been out of order or something?"

"Phone's fine," she said, hauling up the see-through lid to a freezer large enough to store a moose to get some ice. "Just didn't feel like talking to anybody until at least some of the dust settled. And anyway—" she pulled out a carton of lowfat milk and some yogurt from a refrigerator case probably last used for six-packs and stuff "—you and your dad needed some alone time."

"Meaning you didn't want me to know you were pregnant," Rachel said, watching Thea dump milk, ice and yogurt into the blender, her rounded belly clearly visible underneath her white babydoll top. An icy thrill went through Rachel, that soon her tummy would look like that.

"Actually, I didn't," Thea said quietly. "Not yet." Rachel rolled her eyes. "It wasn't personal, Rach, okay?"

"Whatever."

"Hey."

At Thea's sharp tone, Rachel's eyes snapped to hers. "Honey, you know I love you, but I *really* don't need attitude right now. If you hadn't blindsided me with your own news, I would've told you. After I told your father, of course. But you did, and the timing sucked."

"Sorry," Rachel muttered, her face warm, and Thea said, "It's okay, let's move on," and Rachel nodded, taking a deep breath as Thea broke a banana into three pieces and dropped it into the blender.

"How'd you find out, anyway?" Thea asked.

Franny nosed Rachel's hand for more love, while J.D.—short for "Just Dog"—crashed down beside her on his back with his gigundo brown paws in the air. "I overhead Dad and Ozzie talking last night," she said, toying with one of Franny's jackrabbitlike ears. "Although I would've figured it out on my own soon enough. You're, like, *so* showing already."

The blender's roar nixed any further conversation for a minute or so; after Thea turned it off, she said, "Since Miss Manners doesn't say jack about the proper etiquette when a man's daughter and his ex-girlfriend find themselves preggo at the same time, we're all winging it here." She poured the concoction into a tall glass, sprinkled cinnamon on top and poked in a straw. "Here ya go."

Rachel got up and walked over to the counter separating the kitchen from, well, everything else. "You only made one?"

"It's Wednesday, remember?" she said, and Rachel felt a slight pang that she wasn't included in Thea's little circle.

"Oh, yeah. I forgot."

"Hey," Thea said, her voice all soft. "You okay?"

And wasn't that the question of the hour? Who knew you could be this happy and scared and angry all at the same time? "No idea," she finally said, then took a long draw of the sweet, spicy smoothie. "I mean, I'm still okay with being pregnant, even though I know everybody else is ready to string me up. But now you're pregnant, too, except you and Dad aren't together, which really sucks. And Jesse—"

She looked down so Thea wouldn't see her trembling jaw. Usually she was sure everything was going to be fine, but sometimes…

"Have you even heard from him?" Thea gently asked, and Rachel shook her head. "C-could we not talk about him right now?"

"Sure." Moving dogs out of her way, Thea turned back to the sink to wash the blender. Not until it was back on its stand, though, did she say, "How, um, did your dad sound about the baby? His and mine, I mean?"

"Oh, you know Dad," Rachel said, poking holes in the foam. "Like he does about everything. Determined to make the best of it, I guess." She sucked up a tiny bit of banana through the straw, smashing it against the roof of her mouth with her tongue. "Already making noises about turning one of the extra bedrooms into a nursery."

Thea's head snapped around. "For you, you mean?"

"No, I already told him—Jesse and me, we're going to get our own place." *Say it loud enough and you can make it happen.* "So he was definitely talking about your baby. Then Ozzie asked him if he thought he might like a boy this time, and Dad got real quiet for a couple seconds, like he hadn't gotten that far in his thinking yet."

"And…?"

"And he finally said the usual stuff people say, that as long as it was healthy, he didn't care."

And yeah, it stung like hell that not once had Dad said anything like that about *her* baby. At least, not to her. Sure, he said they'd get through it and all, but no matter what Dad said, Rachel knew he was still mad at her. Or at least disappointed. Not that she entirely blamed him, she thought with a sigh. From his standpoint, what else could this look like but one of the dumbest moves ever? It might not've been so bad if Jesse hadn't pulled his disappearing act. Then again, since clearly Jesse wasn't one of Dad's favorite people, maybe not.

Her attention shifted back to Thea, now flopped on her bright yellow-and-white-striped sofa, her lap full of dogs, her mind clearly elsewhere. "You ask me, I think Dad's a lot more up for becoming a father again than he's letting on," she said, and Thea gave her a slightly unfocused look. "Becoming a grandfather, though…no so much."

"Oh, sweetie…" She patted the sofa beside her, muttering, "Not you, doofus," as she shoved Bugly, a creepy-looking, bulgy-eyed chihuahua/pug mix, out of the way to make room for Rachel. When she sank into the thick cushions and leaned into Thea's shoulder, Thea took one of Rachel's hands in both of hers, tiny hands with blunt nails and fingertips nearly as callused as her dad's, as honest and real and unapologetic as the rest of her.

"I swear, there are times I think your dad fell off a horse one too many times," Thea said. Rachel almost smiled. "But I'm sure he'll come 'round. Even if I have to smack 'im around a little to make that happen."

At the image of tiny Thea physically accosting her father, Rachel laughed for the first time in almost a week. Then, as she pulled Bugly into her lap, dodging the thing's nonstop tongue, she gasped out, "Omigod—our kids are gonna go through school together. How weird is that?"

* * *

Pretty damn weird, Thea thought, staring at Norma Jean, blond and plump and wavy-furred, lounging on the chair opposite the sofa, large brown eyes soft with vulnerability. In many ways, Thea idly mused, each of her dogs seemed to incorporate bits of her own personality. Except, perhaps, for Chuck, the huge, mangy beast draped across her lap who looked like his mama had fooled around with a yak.

Speaking of mamas…

"You tell your mother yet?" she asked, handily ignoring the pinch of guilt from having not told hers yet, either.

"Are you serious? Although I guess I'll have to when she's here for graduation. Which reminds me, we got our tickets for the ceremony!"

Poor Bugly dumped off her lap, Rachel fished a ticket out of her purse by the front door and handed it to Thea. Who smiled bravely even though graduation ceremonies ranked right up there with bikini waxes on her Rather Die than Do list. "By that time," Rachel said as she meandered to Thea's worktable, where several brightly painted wooden coyotes waited to be varnished, "Jesse'll be over whatever he's going through, and we'll have some concrete plans, so she can't go all ballistic on us."

Right.

"Dad also told Ozzie he asked you to marry him," Rachel said with the unerring timing of the young, dropping back onto Thea's La-Z-Boy scratch-n-dent bargain sofa. "But you said no."

"I did. And please don't tell me he sent you to soften me up."

"Not hardly." Her eyes stopped rolling long enough to slide to Thea's. "Still. I think you'd be a pretty cool stepmom."

Thea laughed, although it wasn't a happy sound. "Thanks for the vote of confidence, baby. And you'd be a pretty cool stepkid. But your dad and I broke up. For reasons that aren't gonna get fixed just because I'm pregnant."

"But you love him, right?" Rach asked, eyes big and sincere and hopeful, and something like rage surged through Thea, how close she'd come to getting sucked into yet another disaster, followed by bittersweet relief that she hadn't. That, now, she was stronger than the pull.

Even if only just.

"I care about your father a great deal. Obviously," she said with a rueful grin. "But this—" she palmed her belly "—was a curveball. Honey," she said to Rach's confused expression, "people don't get married anymore just because there's a baby coming. Unless they want to, of course." At the girl's heavy silence, Thea laid a hand on her knee. "You can't force somebody to be ready for something like this. Jesse's probably still in shock—"

"Dad's accepted *your* pregnancy!"

"He's also twice Jesse's age. Not to mention responsible to the point of being a pain in the ass," she said dryly. "But as far as your dad and I are concerned, there's no getting around the fact that if we didn't see eye-to-eye on a lot of things before this happened, a baby's not going to make that any easier." At the girl's frown, Thea added, "We had an understanding, Rach. Our relationship…wasn't about love."

"You two just…hooked *up?*"

"Your generation didn't invent the concept. I'm sorry," she said when the girl pulled a totally disgusted face. "I can't sugarcoat it. And I know you wouldn't want me to. Any more than I can sit here and tell you everything's gonna be all right with Jesse. Because I don't know any such thing."

"You don't know Jess," the girl said, her expression stormy as she tightly folded her arms over her still-flat stomach.

"I know that things don't always work out the way we want them to. And I'm sure you don't want to hear that—"

"You're right. I don't."

Thea felt a sudden spurt of sympathy for Johnny. And one of dread for herself. "Honey…Jess is a good kid. And I know there's more to him than your poor father's willing to see. But the prospect of becoming a parent…it's scary, sweet thing. Even when you want it, it's scary."

Rachel's eyes swung to hers. "You wish *you* weren't pregnant?"

A smile pushed at Thea's mouth. "The baby, I want more than anything. But I'm not gonna lie. I wish the circumstances surrounding its conception were different."

After a moment, Rachel laid her head back to stare at the acoustical tiled ceiling. "I've been crazy about babies and kids all my life. I loved babysitting. And I knew I didn't want to be one of those women who waited until she was, like, *old,* before she had kids. But now…" Her mouth thinned. "I really thought Jess and I wanted the same things."

Any time now, Thea thought, somebody else could come in and take over her part of the conversation. "And at any point, did the two of you agree that this would be a good time to make a baby?"

Another blush. "We talked about having kids—"

"When?"

The teen's mouth turned down at the corners. "Jesse told me, if anything happened, he'd be there for me. For us. He did, Thea," she said, tears swelling in her eyes. "I'm not lying!"

"I'm sure you're not," she said, aching for her. "But…honey…boys aren't exactly thinking with their brains at times like that, you know? They make promises they don't even know they're making. Hell, promises they can't even *hear* themselves make on account of all the blood rushing south."

"Not Jesse," Rachel said, mouth set in a stubborn line. "I know he thinks I somehow tricked him, because—like you said—he's scared. But it wasn't like that. And anyway, *I* totally knew what I was getting into. It's not like I'm not taking responsibility for my actions."

"And how do you expect to do that? Especially if you do end up being on your own?"

"That's not gonna happen!" the girl said, jumping to her feet. "Jess'll come around! Maybe he needs time to get used to the idea or whatever, but he'll be back! God, why doesn't anybody understand?" Flinging a chunk of Day-Glo pink hair over her shoulder, she grabbed her purse off the coffee table and bolted across the room, sending dogs scurrying for cover. "I'm gonna be late for work," she muttered, yanking open the door and disappearing through it.

Exhausted, Thea drew her dogs close, thinking she was way too old for so much drama. And definitely way too tired to take on anyone else's. At least, though, she wouldn't have to deal with anybody else when she went to her appointment tomorrow.

Just her and Itty-Bit, all by their lonesome.

Or so she thought, until, at nine the next morning, her doorbell rang.

Chapter Five

"Why aren't you dressed?" Johnny growled when Thea answered the door, looking like a pocket-size hell on a bad day.

"Why are you here?" she said, arms crossed. Loaded for bear.

"You're not going to the doctor alone."

"Says who?"

"You can either come peacefully, or I will pick you up and carry you to the damn office. Your choice."

"You wouldn't."

"You've got ten minutes." He came inside, fending off dogs. Trying not to wince at the abomination the woman called home. All this color couldn't possibly be good for the nervous system. "Just time enough for me to have a cup of that coffee. And why are you drinking coffee, anyway?" he said, moving toward the coffeemaker, set up in her work area rather than the kitchen. More color. His retinas would never forgive him.

"It's decaf. And shouldn't you be worrying about Rachel instead of me?"

"Told you, I'm good at multitasking." He found a mug, checked to make sure it wasn't something she used to mix her paints in, filled it. Tried not to grimace. What the hell was the point of decaf, anyway? "So she's already taken care of, her first appointment's tomorrow. And no, she doesn't know yet. Trust me, it's better this way." When Thea didn't move, Johnny checked his watch, then looked over. "Nine minutes."

"Jerk," Thea muttered, shuffling away. But damned if, eight and half minutes later, they weren't walking out the door.

Had a brief skirmish over him helping her into his truck—of course—but then they were off. Although for sure she wasn't exactly happy, sitting over there on the other side of the bench seat with her arms folded over her middle, frowning out her window.

"You pissed off?" he asked.

"What was your first clue?"

"Only trying to do what's best."

"I'm not one of your mares, Johnny. I'm not one of *your* anythings."

"No, but that is my baby growing inside you. A baby I'm half responsible for. So I'm not gonna apologize for making sure its mama's well taken care of."

"In other words, you didn't trust I'd show up for the appointment."

"That, too."

After a very long silence, she murmured, "You have no idea how terrified I am," and Johnny's heart cracked, knowing what it took for her to admit that. Especially to him.

"No, I guess I don't, not really. Not from your standpoint, anyway. And I knew you'd be mad as hell at me for doing the caveman routine, but...I can't stand not knowing."

He felt her gaze, warm on his face. "Not knowing?"

"If everything's okay," he said, his right hand gripping the steering wheel. He briefly met her puzzled eyes, then faced front again. "Maybe you can shove things to the back of your mind and not think about them—"

"Not *think* about it? God, Johnny—it's all I *do* think about!"

"Deal with it, then. That's where we differ, because I can't…" He took a deep breath. "I have to know what's going on. Good or bad, I have to know."

"You don't understand. You *can't* understand. It's not the same for you. If it turns out… If there's a problem…"

"I get that, Thea," he said steadily, knowing he didn't dare lose his cool. Not now. "But do you really think I wouldn't care, if something went wrong? That…I'd be relieved or something? Because if that's what you think, you know me even less than I thought."

"This from the man who said kids were a pain in the ass."

"Oh, for crying out loud…I've been raising an adolescent girl virtually on my own for the past five years, a girl who's taken loud exception to ninety percent of everything that's come out of my mouth, who then tops things off by getting pregnant. So, yeah, kids are a pain in the ass. That doesn't mean you don't love 'em." His forehead puckered. "You think I don't love Rach?"

Several beats passed before she said, "I know you want to do your best by her," and Johnny's gut flared.

"I love my daughter, Thea. I do. So trust me, when this one—" he aimed a glance at Thea's belly "—cries for three hours straight or throws her first no-holds-barred tantrum or tells you you're mean because you won't let her watch TV until her eyeballs fall out, you're gonna think in terms of pain in the ass, too. When she does something boneheaded, it's gonna tear you up like you wouldn't believe. Then she's gonna go and hug you or make you laugh…" He shook his head, cut his eyes to her, then shrugged.

"So…all that you said about not wanting another kid was a lie?"

"Hell, no. That was before I knew he—or she—was on the way. I mean, you're right, of course it's different for men, we can't feel the kid growing inside us, we have to implant the whole idea in our brains. Once we do, though…" He blew a long, steady breath through his nose. "You think I'm not nervous about this appointment? Hell, my insides feel like a bear had a field day in there." He traded hands on the wheel, flexing the one he'd been using. "But whatever we find out, we'll deal with it together."

She stayed quiet for probably a good half minute before muttering, "Sorry I called you a jerk."

He almost smiled. "S'okay. I didn't take it personally."

After a moment's hesitation, she reached across the seat to link a shaky hand with his, her delicate fingers cold and clammy. Figuring that was Thea's way of saying she was glad he was there, Johnny gently squeezed her hand until the trembling stopped, then held on tight the rest of the way.

Because you know something?

He was glad he was there, too.

"You see that?" Naomi Wilson pointed to a dark spot in the middle of the blurry, undulating image on the sonogram screen. "That's your baby's heart." Ozzie's fifty-something daughter turned to Thea, a broad grin stretched across an unlined face. Behind gold-rimmed glasses, hazel eyes twinkled. "And it's just as strong as can be. Listen."

Transfixed, awestruck, Thea could only stare at the blob that was her baby as his or her heartbeat *whooshwhoosh-whooshwhooshed* through the Doptone Naomi held firmly to

Thea's belly. Johnny's hand, warm and steady, squeezed hers. She glanced up, saw the wonder and relief and amazement in his features, and thought, *Don't get sucked in, princess, it's not about you.* Slipping her hand out of Johnny's, she looked back at the screen.

"He's really okay?"

"He—or she—really is. And so are you," Naomi said, helping her to sit up. "We'll have to wait on the bloodwork to be absolutely sure, of course," Naomi was saying, handing her a tissue to wipe the slimy Doptone goop off her stomach, "but so far, everything looks great. Are you taking your prenatal vitamins?"

"I started as soon as I realized I was pregnant."

"Good—"

"You didn't tell me that," Johnny said, and Thea let out a sigh. Fine, so she'd had a moment, but she was over it now. Mostly. Enough at least to chafe at the idea of his holding her hand—literally—through the poking and prodding part of the program. Last thing she needed was some overprotective macho man flapping around like a daddy eagle protecting his nest.

No, the last thing she needed was her idiotic hormones messing with her head, tempting her to forget that THIS. WASN'T. REAL. That Johnny was only here out of a sense of duty. Even so, what could she do? As he said, the baby was half his, so it wasn't like she could throw him out.

Now, as she tugged down her top, Thea met Johnny's frown with a rueful smile. "Guess I forgot to mention the vitamins. But what with you acting like I didn't have a grain of sense in my head, I guess I got my back up." Tucking her flattened hair behind her ears, she added, "And I'd say it won't happen again, but we all know I'd be lying."

Chuckling, the doctor helped Thea down off the examining table, nodding for her to take a seat in front of her no-frills metal desk, her white coat glowing against pale peach walls dotted with degrees and posters of food pyramids and assorted curled-up fetuses snoozing peacefully inside their cozy quarters. When Johnny sat beside her, crossing his ankle over his knee, the doctor smiled at him.

"My father tells me nobody takes better care of his mares and their babies than you."

Obviously startled, Johnny cleared his throat. "I do my best."

"Then I imagine Thea's waiting so long to start prenatal care really got up your nose."

Thea could feel his smug smile. "You might say."

"And normally I'd agree with you," Naomi said, and Thea thought, *What?* as Johnny said, "Excuse me?"

Smiling, Naomi lifted one hand to cut him off. "Never discount a woman's intuition, especially when it comes to cherishing the seed growing inside her. Especially a woman who's been through what Thea has," she added, reaching across the desk to curve long, smooth fingers around Thea's. "Of course I'd like to see Thea's medical records from Oklahoma, if that's possible. But from what she tells me, and from what I'm seeing now, I feel fairly certain that her previous miscarriages had nothing to do with her."

"Told you," Thea muttered in Johnny's direction, ignoring his mighty sigh in response. Then she frowned. "You saying it might've been Keith?"

"Possibly. Miscarriages as a result of a chromosomal abnormality can be caused by either partner. In which case, there's nothing anyone could have done. Or should have." After another slight squeeze, Naomi let go to lace her fingers, saying to Johnny, "The upshot is, plenty of women do go on to have perfectly healthy, normal pregnancies, even after multiple miscarriages." Then to Thea, "And there's no reason to think you won't be one of them. However…"

The doctor's long, ponytailed dreadlocks swished softly against her back when she ducked her chin slightly to pin Thea's gaze with her own. "You're in my clutches now, missy. And I intend to keep a very close eye on you. With Johnny's help."

"Not a problem," Johnny said. Obviously smirking.

"Now look what you've gone and done," Thea said to Naomi, who grinned. Then she stood and rounded her desk to usher an obviously baffled Johnny to the door.

"And I'll let you get right on it, I promise. But first Mama and I need to have a little talk. So you go on out to the waiting room. Miss Thing will be along shortly."

"Look," Thea said, her breathing going shallow when the doctor shut the door behind her, "I know you're only thinking about what's best for the baby, but I don't need—"

"Yes, you do," Naomi said, quietly but firmly, returning to her desk. "And I'm not just thinking about what's best for the baby, I'm thinking about what's best for *you*. What I want to know is why you're not counting your lucky stars your baby's daddy gives a damn."

"Hey. I thought doctors were too busy these days to get involved in their patients' personal business."

"Guess I never got that memo."

Thea blew out a sigh. "I know I'm lucky, Naomi. I really do. At least, as far as Johnny's stepping up to the plate about the baby goes. But we're not together. As a couple, I mean."

"Oh, I know that." Naomi leaned against the front of her desk, her arms folded across her chest. "What I don't know is why."

"Why does any couple break up? You realize it's not going to work, you move on."

"Except every hormone running through your body is trying its level best to make you bond with your baby's daddy." One brow lifted. "Am I right?"

Thea flushed. "I don't want—"

"You don't *want,* you don't *need...*" The doctor shook her head. "Are you listening to yourself?"

Yeah, I'm listening, Thea thought. Listening to the lies a woman tells herself as a distraction from the relentless yearning pulsing steadily, almost painfully, inside her. Tucked deep inside, Itty-Bit fluttered, as if trying to comfort his or her mama. Last night was the first time she'd felt the baby move, even though she mistook it for a gas bubble at first. When she realized, no, it was the real thing, she'd gotten all weepy. And pissed, that she was all alone, with nobody to share the moment.

Now she stroked her tummy, soothing right back. "Enough people let you down over the years, you learn the only person you can ever truly depend on is yourself."

"Oh, I hear you on that," the doctor said, her face folding into a sympathetic frown. "I take it your ex wasn't very supportive during your previous pregnancies?"

"There's an understatement."

"So now you're assuming you can't depend on Johnny, either."

"To do what he's *supposed* to do? Of course. He's nothing like my ex. Nothing. Heck, I'd trust Johnny with my life."

"Just not your heart."

Thea let out a dry laugh. "That works both ways, you know."

"Yes, it does," Naomi said, far too quickly for Thea's peace of mind. "How's your mama?"

Startled, Thea said, "Um...doing okay, I suppose. She remarried some time ago, lives up in Colorado with her husband. Ed. We don't... Our lives don't intersect all that much anymore. Why?"

"She know about the baby?"

"Not yet. I thought I'd hold off until...until I was sure. This time."

After a second or two, Naomi said, "What that woman went through with your father…that was rough, honey. Is she happy now?"

"Far as I know. Ed seems like a decent guy."

"Good. As for Johnny…" The doctor's lips curved. "He's had it pretty rough, too, from everything I hear. My father's not exactly what you'd call circumspect," she added when Thea frowned. "I already knew about Johnny's messed-up childhood, of course, with his daddy taking off and all, how hard his mama had it on her own. But Pop told me how devastated Johnny was when his marriage fell apart, too. How he blamed himself. That's a lot of baggage to be lugging around."

"Naomi…not to be rude or anything, but is there a point to all this?"

The doctor was quiet for several seconds before saying, "Don't shut Johnny out, Thea. No matter how much you want to. It's not fair to the child. Or him. Or even, though I know you don't want to hear this, to you."

After a few seconds' standoff, Thea bent down to pick up her purse from the floor beside the chair. "It wasn't me who shut *him* out," she said, then headed toward the door. But the doctor blocked her exit, her hands gently clamping around Thea's shoulders.

"I do hear you, honey," she said, sympathy heavy in her eyes. "And I don't blame you for trying to save your hide—"

"Then please don't tell me to suck it up, to do what women have been doing forever—" Thea's eyes stung "—to be the generous one, the understanding one…the long-suffering one—"

"And if I thought Johnny was even remotely like your father or your ex, I'd be the first one to tell you to run as far and as fast as those tiny feet of yours can go and not look back. But he's not. And he deserves somebody to be there for him the same way he's willing to be there for you. Not that he'd ever admit it—what man does?—but from what Pop says, Johnny's so used to thinking he's supposed to take care of everybody and everything he won't even notice he's in over his head until he drowns. And you do *not* want that to happen."

Blinking, Thea looked away, at all those pictures of unborn babies, trusting and helpless and oblivious to whatever their parents might be going through. She thought about Keith, who'd never wanted to go with her to her appointments, especially after the first miscarriage. He'd been excited enough, in his own way, when she'd initially become pregnant, an excitement that quickly dissolved into anger and accusation when it didn't take, like it had all been her fault. Looking back, Thea supposed she'd tried so hard to get pregnant again—and again—just to make things right between them. Of course now she understood that things had never been right, but at the time she'd been too young and naive to understand that.

So here she was, pregnant by a man who did care. A good man, an honest man, a man who couldn't help how he felt any more than she could.

A man who was still suffering from the fallout from asking another woman he'd accidentally gotten pregnant to marry him.

Her mouth twisted, Thea returned the doctor's gaze. "I suppose you want me to quit working, too."

That merited an understanding smile. "As long as there aren't any changes and you feel good, I see no reason why you can't keep on the way you've been, at least for the time being. You watching what you eat?"

"It doesn't stick around long enough to watch. Honestly, I'm eating anything that isn't nailed down."

The doctor laughed. "And isn't it always the littlest mamas who end up with the eight-pound babies?"

"Don't even *say* that!"

Chuckling, Naomi opened the door to the waiting room, where Winnie and her husband, Aidan, holding hands, sat chatting with Johnny. Who got to his feet the moment he saw Thea, fists full of cowboy hat, eyes full of concern, and Thea's heart started up like a puppy in a pet-store window, whining and scratching at the glass.

No, no, honey, not this one, she told her heart, because while the concern was genuine enough, unfortunately it was all tangled up in a whole mess of *musts* and *have-tos* and *becauses*…snares that would eventually choke the life out of the concern.

"Play nice," the doctor whispered, even so. Thea grunted a nonresponse—safer that way—then smiled for Aidan and Winnie, who bounded out of her seat to give Thea a warm hug.

"Well?"

"Everything's fine," Thea said, and Winnie squealed a "Yes!!!" and hugged her again. Over her friend's shoulder, Thea caught the expression on Aidan's face as he watched his wife. And although the Irishman's mouth might have twitched with bemusement, there was no mistaking the I-don't-give-a-damn-who-knows-it love shining in his eyes.

A look Thea'd never seen in a man's eyes for her. Not from her ex, God knows, not from Johnny, not from anybody. A thought that didn't make her sad as much as it made her even more determined not to marry anybody unless and until she did.

Oh, yay, a goal, she thought, feeling marginally better.

After the couple disappeared into Naomi's office, Johnny opened the outer office door for Thea, the gallant, honorable cowboy—or reasonable facsimile thereof—at her service, and Naomi's charge to not shut him out scampered through her brain, yapping at her like a freaked Chihuahua.

"So what'd Naomi say?" Johnny asked, his hand on her elbow, warm and steady and sure. Thea's eyes shot to his, catching the sheepish grin, and she thought, *How do I* do *this?* How could she be the friend he needed—the friend who, despite everything, she still wanted to be—without destroying the still-gossamer-thin shell she'd only just erected around her battered heart?

And damned if she didn't see her own ambivalence mirrored in those tortured brown eyes. Gently, she removed her elbow from his grip.

"That I don't have to quit my job," she said, ramming her sunglasses on before the sun blinded her.

Whoever decided it would be a good idea to hold a graduation ceremony outside at the end of May, Johnny thought irritably as the white ball of fire overhead seared his back through his brand-new white dress shirt, *should be taken out and shot.*

Crossing his arms, he shifted his numb butt on the hard wooden seat as his gaze raked the sea of cowboy and floppy-brimmed straw hats around him, trying to figure out which one Thea—whose obviously pained attempts at keeping him "in the loop" were seriously beginning to piss him off—might be hiding under. Trying to ignore the stares and whispers from people realizing that, yeah, that really was Kat Griego sitting next to him. *You know, honey, that lady we see on the news all the time? The one who spent that whole week reporting about those poor little starving children in…where was that again? Someplace in Africa, wasn't it? Strange to think she graduated right from this very high school…*

Not that Kat went out of her way to call attention to herself. In that beige, sleeveless dress and flat sandals—which put her a couple inches shorter than him—she wasn't exactly standing out from the crowd. Except with her high cheekbones and short red hair she was one helluva striking woman. Hard to miss. Hard to forget who she was. Who she'd been.

Who she used to be married to.

Damn, was the air still as death or what? And how long could it take to read off fifty names?

As if on cue, Kat leaned slightly in his direction, her familiar light perfume—stronger smelling in the heat—stirring up the faint aftertaste of arousal, the fine, dry dust of disappointment wedged in those corners of his memory he couldn't quite reach.

"Big day," Kat said.

"Uh-huh."

"Hard to believe our little girl's about to go to college."

Johnny pretended to check his cell for messages. "Mare about to foal," he lied, slipping it back onto the clip on his belt.

Silence.

"Is Rach all right?" Kat whispered on an Altoid-scented wave. "She seems a little subdued."

"She's fine," Johnny grumbled, earning him a brief frown from behind sunglasses large enough to double as satellite TV dishes. Somehow, he didn't think this was the time or place to mention the morning sickness. Which far as he could tell lasted until nearly sunset.

The satellite dishes faced forward again. As did, he imagined, the frown. "She hasn't talked about Jesse once since I've been here. Is…everything okay between them?"

Johnny could hardly contain his smile, tight though it may have been. The one time Kat had met Jesse, about a year ago, she'd nearly choked on her horror. So it didn't take a genius to hear the unspoken *Please tell me that's history* behind her words now. Or, he had to admit, the genuine concern for their daughter, whose asking if she could come live with Johnny full-time had deeply hurt a woman with conflicting loyalties.

He shifted again in his chair, his arms folded. "They're having some problems."

As in, the boy hadn't been out to the house once since the blowup. And every time Johnny brought up the subject, Rach would give him the teary "I don't want to talk about it" routine. So he'd finally given up, figuring his daughter, like her daddy, would talk when she was good and ready and not a minute before.

So why couldn't he shake this I-let-her-down feeling?

Of course, Kat had no idea she was about to become a grandmother. Or that Rachel wasn't going on to college. That little funfest awaited them after the ceremony. The crowning touch, Johnny mused, to a truly lousy couple of weeks where it seemed like nothing pregnant wanted anything to do with him, mares included. Nothing got up his butt worse than an unresolved problem. And right now, that's all his life was—one big, fat, never-ending, unresolved problem.

"You think it's over between them?" his ex whispered, fanning herself with her program.

"Couldn't tell ya," he muttered, ambivalent and hating it. For two years, he'd wanted nothing more than to hear, "Daddy…Jess and I broke up." Now that Rach was pregnant, however…

True, maybe she hadn't exactly played by the rules, but she hadn't been playing by herself, either. Only thing that'd kept him from flushing out the knucklehead and dragging him back to the ranch by his 'nads to face facts had been Thea's reminding him that the kids needed to fix their own mess, meaning Johnny had to stay out of their way—

"Why didn't she say anything to me?" Kat said, and Johnny—whose stash of good humor was about all used up—muttered, "Maybe because there's not much you can do from halfway around the world?"

"Don't even go there, Johnny," Kat said under her breath.

"Both of you know damn well I'm always accessible—even if my cell isn't working, there's always e-mail. She knows she can talk to me anytime."

Johnny wasn't about to argue the point. Especially when he finally spotted Thea, sitting four rows ahead on the aisle in some sacklike floral dress and high-heeled sandals that made her bare feet look sexy as hell. And just like that, all manner of inappropriate thoughts exploded in his brain, and those feet and Kat's perfume started up a tug-of-war in his brain, except the feet won out in about two seconds flat.

Because Kat's perfume was part of his past and Thea's feet were—

Sure as hell not part of his future.

Clearing his throat, he forced his gaze up to bare shoulders shadowed by a large-brimmed, bright pink hat as big as an umbrella. The shoulders—freckled and smooth and smelling like flowers, most likely—did nothing to still his rampaging sex drive, but that dumb hat took the edge off, some. Not enough, but a little. From this angle he couldn't tell how much she was showing, a thought that sent a surge of combined annoyance and worry through him to get all tangled up with the sex thoughts—

"Oh, there's Rach!" Kat said, poking him, and Johnny stuck his fingers in his mouth, letting out a whistle shrill enough to earn him glares from everyone in a twenty-foot radius. Even Thea briefly twisted around, just long enough for him to catch the eye roll and the corners of her glossy mouth twitching—

Another poke. "Who's the woman in the pink hat?"

"Thea Benedict. Don't think you know her." And Kat definitely didn't know *about* her, because talking to each other about their postdivorce relationships wasn't something they did. He frowned, irritated, when a motorcycle's roar cut through the drone of the principal's voice and the faint, almost constant applause.

But Kat was still focused on Thea. "No, actually, I remember her from when I was here the last time. She's a waitress at Ortega's, right? Outgoing, always making jokes?"

"Yeah, I s'pose—"

"RACH-*EL!*" bellowed a male voice from the back of the crowd, and two hundred heads snapped around to see the bald, tattooed dude with his hands cupped around his mouth, and Johnny muttered, "Oh, hell," an instant before his daughter—still onstage, her brand-new diploma clutched in her hand, shrieked, "Jesse?"

"Jesse?" Kat said, as Johnny caught Thea's eyes for one impossibly short moment before Jessie yelled—yes, so everybody and God could hear—"I'm so sorry, baby! You know I love you, but I got all crazy—"

"It's okay!" Rachel screamed, beaming, overjoyed, *clueless,* her graduation gown wadded in her fists as she clomped down the steps toward her boyfriend, yelling that she loved him, too, and Johnny, knowing what was coming, thought, *No, not okay, not okay at all,* but there wasn't a damn thing he could do to stop it, short of mowing down everybody between here and the aisle and launching himself at the boy—

Who, in the middle of the aisle, lifted his daughter off her platform-shoed feet and swung her around, both of them laughing like idiots. Then in one clumsy, but oddly efficient, motion, Jesse set her down, lowered himself to one knee and held out a ring box.

"Will you marry me, Rach?" he asked, over her shrieking, and she said, "Omigod, *yes!*" and Johnny heard Kat's sharp breath, felt her fingers dig into his shoulder, caught the *I'm so sorry* in Thea's eyes.

Then Jesse stood, grinning, his beefy arm clamped around Rachel's slender waist, and yelled out, "Hey, everybody! *I'm gonna be a daddy!*"

"That's a joke, right?" Kat said behind him, probably not grinning, as Johnny lowered his face into his palms and wished the sun would incinerate him altogether.

Chapter Six

Well, gee, wasn't that *fun?* Thea thought as she wriggled her way through the clot of hot, thrilled parents and their white-gowned, pimply-faced progeny in her quest for the nearest toilet. If nothing else, the lovebirds' public reconciliation had temporarily halted the eyebrow-raising epidemic among those who'd clearly been vacationing on Mars and hadn't heard about her pregnancy. The '60s tent-dress pattern might have been big enough to smuggle the family silver under, but not, apparently, a not-quite-five-months-along baby bump.

The building was open, praise be, the high-ceilinged interior as musty and cool as she remembered from nearly twenty years ago. Her sandals clickety-clacked over the worn tile flooring as she hotfooted it to the girls' bathroom, which was mercifully empty. A few minutes later she emerged from the stall, much relieved, to see Rachel vanish into the next stall over like a ghost with Bill Murray on her heels.

And the day just kept getting better.

"Another ten seconds," the girl called out from the stall, ecstatic as all hell, "and I swear I would've wet my pants—"

"Rachel!" Kat Griego yelled as she shoved open the door to the girls' room. "Don't you dare run away from me! Oh!" She stopped short when she caught sight of Thea, a half smile flitting across reddened cheeks. "Sorry! I didn't realize anyone else was in here."

"No problem, I'm on my way out—"

"Thea! No!" The toilet flushed and Rachel flew out to grab Thea's hand, eyes huge. Pleading. "Don't go!"

Yeah, the trapped-bunny feeling was just what Thea needed. "Honey, this has nothing to do with me," Thea said, wriggling free. "Your mom and you need to talk about this in private—"

So naturally some middle-aged gal Thea didn't know picked that moment to escort an ancient comma of a woman, claws firmly clamped around her walker, into the bathroom, the pair chattering in loud, incomprehensible Spanish.

"Let's go, Rachel," Kat said, over the chattering and stall doors banging open, her voice calm but her entire body bristling with the same restless energy Thea dimly remembered from their high school days, when Kat was still Katie. Not that their paths had crossed much, with Thea being a freshman and Kat a senior, but even then it was obvious the redhead couldn't wait to blow this joint. "Your father's waiting—"

"Tell her, Thea," Rachel said, grabbing her hand again. "Tell her how good Jess and I are together, that this isn't a bad thing!"

"Oh, no, you are *not* putting me in the middle of this," Thea said, which got a shocked, hurt look from Rachel and a shrewd one from her mother. And a slight frown aimed at Thea's baby bulge. "You're old enough to make a baby, to get married, you're old enough to deal with the consequences of your decision."

"But you heard him," Rachel said, clearly ignoring her, "everybody heard him—"

"Ain't that the truth," Kat muttered, and Thea bit her lip.

"He's really, *really* sorry, he just needed to work out a few things in his head, like you said, and—"

"And you're *seventeen,* Rachel," Kat said, clearly not caring anymore about privacy. "College, a career…all of it thrown away, for what? *Good* is definitely *not* the word I'd use to describe this!"

"It's *my* life, Mom! Which you've never, not once, understood! I—" On a groan, she bolted back toward the stall, nearly taking out the old crone's walker in the process. Retching noises ensued. Kat looked at Thea, her gaze again slipping to Thea's middle.

"Why do I get the feeling there's more to this story than I'm seeing?"

Thinking *Why me?,* Thea dug in her purse for her Tic Tacs even as she offered a reassuring smile for Walker Woman and her sidekick as they headed out. Another flush, then Rachel wobbled back to the sink, looking slightly green. Thea handed her a paper cup full of water and a Tic Tac. Wordlessly, Rachel took both, staring into the cup of water as if it would tell her the future.

"Does this really go away eventually?"

"Yes," Kat said on a sigh, and Thea said, "For what it's worth I'm down to one barf a day."

"Lucky," Rachel mumbled, spitting out her rinse water into the sink, then popping in the mint.

"Eating helps."

A hand clamped over her mouth, the girl vanished into the stall again. When she returned, Thea and Kat made her sit on one of the cigarette-burn-dotted vinyl chairs that predated *their* high school days. Over a resolute chin, runny brown eyes peered up at Thea. And in them, Thea was startled to see something far more solid and sure than plain old childish stubbornness.

"You don't believe Jess and I can make a go of this, do you? You never did."

Thea glanced at Kat, frowning at her daughter, then said, "It's like your mom said, honey, you're seventeen—"

"Eighteen. Next month."

"Even so," Kate said. "The odds are still seriously stacked against you—"

"Just like the odds were seriously stacked against a small-town girl from New Mexico becoming a world-class journalist?" Rachel said quietly. Reasonably.

Thea saw the other woman pale. "It's not the same thing."

"That's right, it's not. I'm not. I don't want what you wanted, Mom. I never did. And I know this isn't going to be easy. It already isn't—hurling every five minutes isn't exactly my idea of a fun time, okay? Look, Jess and I haven't had a chance to really talk about this. Right now, all I have is his apology. And the fact that he came back for me. He didn't have to, but he did. That has to count for something, doesn't it?"

"And if it doesn't work out?" her mother said, her voice trembling slightly. "You'll have no education, nothing to fall back on. What are you going to do then?"

"I never said I wasn't going to continue my education. Plenty of moms go to college after they have their babies. But the thing is…I have no clue what to study yet. I do know I want to be a mom. And I know I want to stay right here, not go off somewhere to 'broaden my horizons.' I got enough of a peek at those horizons with you, Mom, to know…they're not me."

On that note, the girl got to her wobbly feet and looked from Thea to her mom and back again. "Just because neither of you could work things out with Dad doesn't mean Jesse and I won't. So how about backing off and giving us that chance, huh?"

Then she clumped out of the bathroom, her gown billowing behind her.

Silence buzzed between Thea and Kat for several seconds until Kat finally said, "Your baby—"

"Yep. Johnny's."

"Dear God." A strangled sound sputtered from Kat's mouth. "I don't know whether to laugh or cry."

"Tell me about it," Thea said.

"I'd forgotten how beautiful it is up here," Kat said, accepting the chilled tallneck Johnny held out for her. The old floorboards creaked when she settled back again, propping her sandaled feet on the top of the porch railing, and Johnny thought how out of place she looked. And probably felt. Even so, after their daughter's bombshell Kat had canceled whatever her plans had been, checked out of her tony Santa Fe hotel and laid claim to one of the guestrooms. So here she was, sitting on his porch, drinking his beer, reminding him of how badly things can go wrong. Especially when she said, "Makes me almost forget the rest of the world even exists."

In the rocker next to hers, Johnny hunched forward, rolling his own beer between his palms. "The key word being *almost*," he said quietly, tilting the bottle to his lips.

"It's my life," his ex said, just as quietly, sounding exactly like their daughter. But not nearly as defensively as she might've at one time. "If it weren't for the wedding I wouldn't even be here."

As it had every time the subject had come up over the past four days, the word stung like a whip, even if Johnny was doing his best to yield to the inevitable with as much grace as he had in him. From the tense conversation with Jesse on graduation night, when the kid made his case for marrying

Rachel with an eloquence and passion that, truth be told, had jarred loose more than a little respect for his determination, to a solution to their housing problem Johnny couldn't've possibly have foreseen, he felt like he was whitewater rafting down a raging river, miraculously dodging rock after rock.

And all he could do was hang on for the ride.

"We have to give them their chance, Katie," he said, reverting to the name he'd called her all those years ago, when he'd believed if he just loved her enough, he'd *be* enough. That nothing would ever mess up what they had.

"Like we had ours?"

Johnny twisted around to look at Kat, watching the sun slip behind the mountains, leaching the last bit of color from the sky. "They're not us."

Laying her head back, Kat laughed. "No. They certainly aren't."

"Look…I don't feel any better about this than you do, believe me, but…" He thought of Thea's words that day, before he'd known she was also pregnant, which in turn provoked a twist of guilt, that everything'd been so crazy since the graduation he'd hardly touched base with her, to make sure she was okay. She was fine, of course. In fact, she was going to be Rachel's maid of honor. "But they're gonna need our help. To get through this. They know this isn't the choice we would've made for them, but for the sake of our grandbaby, if nothing else, we've gotta stand by 'em."

Kat took a swallow of her own beer, then propped the bottle on her blue-jeaned thigh, her silence burrowing into his skull. Johnny blew out an exasperated sigh.

"Why don't you just come right out and say what you're thinking, Kat? That I could've prevented this."

Her eyes cut to his. "You really think I'm that petty? Or worse, naive? Of course I don't blame you. Not that the thought didn't cross my mind, but that's because society generally frowns on throttling pregnant teenagers, which would've been my first impulse. Sure, I'm angry—no secret there—but I'm hardly one to throw stones, am I?"

"You weren't seventeen."

"I still listened to my heart instead of my head."

"You sure about that?"

Kat took another sip of her beer. "I did love you, Johnny. Then, I mean. And afterward...I wanted it to work. I really did."

"But you couldn't help who you were. Any more than Rach can help who she is."

Soft laughter, carried on the evening breeze, interrupted whatever Kat had been about to say. Jess and Rach came into view, walking hand in hand down to the nearest pasture, which was bright green from a recent rain. Three days from now, they'd be married, in a ceremony barely one step up from a Vegas elopement, minus the slot machines and the Elvis impersonator. Their hands still linked, Jess looped his arm around Rachel's waist and leaned over to kiss the top of her head, the gesture gentle and affectionate and settled, somehow, and Johnny's throat closed around the scream fighting to escape, even as the thought of going through this all over again, with another kid, clenched his stomach.

And yet, through all of that trickled something that felt an awful lot like...envy. For what, he wasn't sure. Their innocence, maybe. Not of the body, obviously, but their hope, smooth and unscuffed as a new pair of boots.

God, he felt old.

Beside him, Kat stretched, gently tapping her beer bottle on her knee. "She's so damn bright, Johnny," she said, her words weighted with equal parts sadness and resignation. "All the options she had—"

"Unfortunately, she chose one you didn't think of."

"How could she possibly know what she really wants?"

"You did," Johnny said, taking some small satisfaction when she didn't argue with him. "Unfortunately, I was too young and stupid and blinded by all that red hair—" he smiled when Kat chuckled "—to get it through my thick head that I'd never be a decent substitute for that. Katie—I was fine with whatever you wanted for Rach, as long as that's what she wanted, too. And I think, for a long time, to please you, she tried to shoehorn herself into your vision for her. But shoehorning didn't work for her any more than it did for you."

His ex pushed a slender hand through her short hair, let her palm slap onto the rocker arm. "I should've realized…" Her gaze swung to Johnny. "Rach was miserable in New York. Especially after her visits out here. Even when she'd travel with me…" She laughed softly. "Paris was lost on her. Still…" She rubbed her wrist into the wood, then clamped both hands around her bottle. "The thought of her getting trapped…"

"Like we said. She's not you."

A long moment later she said, "I'm so sorry—"

"It was a million years ago. Forget it." He watched the young couple, leaning on the cracked, split-rail fence he'd been meaning to fix for years, Rachel feeding carrots to one of the horses, her entire body conveying her contentment and happiness. "I guess it comes down to figuring out where we really belong, Kat," Johnny said in a rare philosophical moment. "Who we are. Maybe instead of worrying we should be grateful Rachel figured it out so early. *And* had the guts to act on it."

"And if she changes her mind?"

Johnny smiled. "If it's one thing Rach isn't, it's flighty. Pigheaded, yes. But I've never known anybody more comfortable in her own skin." *Besides Thea,* he thought, starting from the ambush. "Some people spend years trying to find themselves. If they ever do. Seems to me Rach knew from birth exactly who she was. What she wanted."

"Good point," Kat said on a rush of air, lowering one foot to the porch floor. The bottle clunked softly against the floorboards as she set it down. "So. You really ready to raise another child?"

Johnny scratched his back against the chair's slats. "You know, if you'd asked me that a month ago, I would've laughed you right off this porch. Wasn't exactly excited about the prospect when I first found out, either. But you know...I missed so much of Rach's growing up. She'd get off the plane after months with you, and I'd think, damn, who *is* this?"

"You *let* me take her away, Johnny—"

"I know. And I'm not blaming you." His arms crossed high on his chest, he frowned over at her. "This wasn't enough for you, and I knew that. Knew it all along, even if I didn't want to admit it. And Rach was just a little thing, she needed to be with her mama." He looked away again. "But don't think it wasn't hard, letting her go. And then having to get to know her all over again every few months..." His jaw clenched, he shook his head.

"I'm sorry," Kat said again.

"Nothing to be sorry for. Stuff happens, we make the best of it and move on. But I'm kinda looking forward to being around this one all the time."

Kat shifted in her chair. "But I thought you and Thea weren't together?"

"I'm thinking the baby changes things on that score."

"And I'm gathering Thea doesn't agree with you. Rach said you asked her to marry you," Kat said, the unspoken "too" twanging between them like an off-tune guitar string. "But she turned you down."

His eyes slid to Kat's. "That doesn't mean I intend to

stop trying. In the meantime, at least I know Thea's not going anywhere."

Except the words no sooner left his mouth than uncertainty smacked him upside the head. Because, as he said, stuff happened. Thea'd left Tierra Rosa once before; what's to say she wouldn't leave again?

"You love her?"

Johnny looked over at his ex, who'd twisted slightly to hike one foot onto the rocker's seat, her elbow propped on her knee.

"Does it matter?"

"Not to me, no," Kat said, like she was finding this funny as all get-out. Then, her expression softer, she leaned over, touched his arm. "I do want you to be happy, Johnny. I always have. Which is why it tore me up inside when things fell apart between us. Maybe you don't believe that, but—"

"No, I believe it." And that was no lie. He knew Kat'd been just as miserable about the breakup as he had. For different reasons, maybe, but still. Knowing that didn't help matters any—if anything, it only made things worse—but it had gone a long way toward keeping the lines of communication open about their daughter. Now she gently squeezed his arm, the fading light barely enough for him to see the real enough concern in her gray eyes.

"Loneliness is a bitch, Johnny. So. Do you love her?"

Johnny snapped his head back around, her words like acid on an open wound. Lonely? Hell, yeah, he knew all about lonely, about how, no matter how busy you kept your days, it would creep back every night to plaster itself up against you like a big, smelly dog. About how, since Thea'd left, the dog seemed bigger and smellier than ever. And even less inclined to go annoy somebody else.

"I care about her," he said, irritably. "And I want to do what's right. Why can't that be enough?"

"Oh, Johnny," Kat said, the heavy dusk swallowing her sigh.

* * *

Surreal, that was the only word for it, Thea decided as she hung back by the refreshments table, watching the newlyweds up on the porch, opening their wedding presents and gleefully flouting every convention known to wedding planners the world over. But since there'd been no time for a shower *and* a wedding, the general consensus had been *What the hell—let 'em have their fun.*

Which made perfect sense being as both bride and groom were wearing blue jeans and cowboy boots, as were the parents of the bride and probably half the guests. At least the bride could still *get* into her jeans—Thea had finally given up the good fight two weeks ago, breathing a sigh of relief when Rach had said the dress Thea'd worn to her graduation would be fine. Even if she looked like she was wearing a lampshade.

She stuffed another mini-quiche into her mouth to make herself feel better.

"You might want to think about leaving some for everybody else," Ozzie said beside her, the slight breeze rustling the white banquet cloth he'd magically produced. Overhead, a benign sun beamed in a cloudless blue sky; birds twittered and flowers bloomed and horses dozed in bright green pastures. Like having a wedding in Teletubbies land.

"Hey. They know where the food is. And they know there's a pregnant woman in their midst. You snooze, you lose." As the old man chuckled, Thea nodded toward the cake, a three-layer, triple-chocolate masterpiece. "That, Ozzie, is freaking amazing."

"And I don't want you even smellin' it until the bride cuts it." Thea stuck her tongue out at him and dispatched another quiche. Another chuckle, behind her—a younger, female version of Ozzie's—sent guilt whizzing through her widdle veins.

Slipping a warm arm around Thea's waist, Naomi said, "They sure look happy, don't they?"

"Mmm," Thea said, eyes peeled for an escape route.

"You know," the doctor said with an affectionate glance at Ozzie, busy plugging the holes in the goody platters where Thea'd ravaged them, "Pop wasn't much older than that when he married Mama. Twenty, maybe. Mama was sixteen. They had nearly sixty years together before she passed. So it can work."

"Times were different then."

"Love's not." Naomi let go to filch a stuffed mushroom, her gaze scanning the crowd—such as it was—as she munched. "You and Johnny been talking?"

"He's been busy."

The older woman looked at Thea, her eyes crinkled. "His ex being here has nothing to do with the two of you."

"There is no 'two of us,' Naomi—"

"And soon there's going to be a *three* of you."

Ignoring Ozzie's wheezy laugh, Thea longingly eyed the cake. Then her gaze shifted to Johnny, all gussied up in a right-out-of-the-package Western shirt—she could see the creases from here, pathetic—and a bolo tie, leaning against the porch railing with his arms crossed, focused on his daughter and new son-in-law. Speaking of things she couldn't have. Not really. Although at least she'd get some of the cake. Eventually.

Kat stood a few feet away, feet apart, hands shoved in the pockets of her white linen capris, her neck and wrists suffocated with enough turquoise and silver jewelry to keep a reservation afloat for months. Although Kat was hardly one of those Stepford anchors with Barbie hair and phosphorescent teeth, Thea sincerely doubted the woman whacked off her own tresses with a pair of sewing shears, or gouged out the last little bit of lipstick with her pinky finger, or considered shopping at Macy's instead of Target a splurge.

"That's who he fell in love with, Naomi. Kind of a hard act to follow, doncha think?" As though he'd heard her, Johnny turned, frowning slightly in her direction, and Thea's stomach turned inside out. Or would have if Itty-Bit hadn't been in the way. It wasn't an idle, unseeing glance, either. Oh, no—that half smile and slight nod were definitely for her.

Speaking of surreal. All these people, all this hoopla, all this strangeness writhing between them, and yet there was no denying this…this *intimacy* that was completely apart from what they'd done to make this baby—

And, man, was it quiet beside her or what? Frowning, she turned. "What?"

"One, that's *not* who he fell in love with. That's who she turned into. Two, I'm thinking she's not exactly competition, seeing as they got divorced fifteen years ago—"

"Yeah, well, if you want to get all logical about it—"

"—and three, for somebody that convinced that there's no 'two of you,' that was some serious wordless communication going on there."

"I never said there wasn't a bond. Just not the right kind of bond—"

"And this one's from Naomi!" Rachel called out, looking about to burst with happiness as Jesse—grinning like a goofball himself—held aloft yet another silver-and-white-wrapped something or other. The last of their loot, apparently.

"You know what they say about weddings being infectious," the doctor said with a grin, then hiked up her long, brightly patterned skirt to troop up to the porch.

"Geez, she's worse than you are," Thea muttered to Ozzie, who just shrugged.

The wedding presents duly opened and admired, the

buzzing, chattering crowd descended upon the buffet table. Suddenly weary, Thea headed back toward the house, where it would be cooler, quieter, and most important of all, devoid of humanity.

"Thea! Wait up a sec."

Almost, she thought wearily as she turned to see Jesse heading up the hill toward her. Alone. Wary, she shoved her blowing hair out of her eyes. "Hey, Jess—what's up?"

"I've hardly had a chance to talk to you," the kid said, panting slightly when he reached her. He grinned, showing off a set of dimples that completely shot the bad-boy image. "To say thanks for all your help over the last week. With the wedding and stuff. It turned out real nice. Thanks."

The heartfelt compliment made her blush. By rights, that privilege should have fallen to Rachel's mother, but it had quickly become clear that Thea was a lot better than Kat at pulling together a wedding out of thin air. "You're welcome, Jess. It was my pleasure. How's the move coming?"

Turned out part of Naomi's decision to move back to Tierra Rosa hinged on coaxing her eighty-four-year-old father into both semiretirement and her brand-new, two-bedroom condo. Naturally, Ozzie'd resisted her suggestions with everything he had in him…until he decided it was downright selfish to stay on in the old cabin when here was this young couple who needed a place to live.

"Good. Who knew Rach would be totally cool with living so close to her dad?" A large hand streaked over his freshly shaved head before earnest eyes met hers. "Rach thinks the world of you, Thea. So I just want to make sure…you're okay with this. We know it's not gonna be easy, but we'll be okay."

"Jesse," Thea said gently, "a month ago you ran out because you were scared—"

"So how's anybody supposed to trust I won't run again? I

know what you're thinking, and I don't blame you. Yeah, I was scared. Still am, if you wanna know the truth. So's Rach, even if she won't admit it. But I love her, Thea, I really do." He grinned. "Don't get me wrong, she doesn't let me get away with crap. But she doesn't go around ragging on me, either, like I see a lot of the girls do to their boyfriends. She's always just...herself, you know? And she lets *me* be myself, too..."

Rachel's laughter carried to them on the breeze. Jesse twisted around to look at her, sitting cross-legged in the grass with Baby Julia on her lap, and Miguel and Robbie on either side of her, the boys giggling when the squealing baby tried to grab their noses. "She's *happy,* Thea. Happier than I've ever seen her."

"It's her wedding day, of course she's happy. It's all the days from now on that are going to be the challenge."

Letting out a growl—of frustration with her, Thea imagined—Jess lowered himself onto the top porch step, his eyes on the scene below. "Ozzie and his wife were real young when they got married, too. Did you know that?"

"Yeah. Naomi told me."

"He said in some ways they probably had it easier, because they were too young to really know what they were getting into. That the older people are when they get married, the more they worry about everything that can go wrong."

Chuckling softly, Thea sat beside him, deciding not even she could bring herself to burst the poor guy's bubble on his wedding day. "Can't argue with him there."

"I know everybody's worried about how we're gonna get by, especially after the baby comes. But see, while I was away, I was busy getting my sh—um, act together. Coming up with a plan. Rach might only be thinking of now, but I'm thinking about the future. Our future, as a family.

"So for now," he said, "I'm gonna take on more of the cabinetmaking so my brother can concentrate on his furniture, and that's steady work. But Eli's never been interested in growing the family business, and I am. So I think maybe I'll take some marketing courses and stuff, see what's up with that. And like I already told Rach's mom, I'll make sure she goes to college, when she's ready. Because no matter what she says now, one day she's gonna want to do that. And damned if I'm gonna stand in her way—"

"There you are!"

They looked up to see Rach approaching them, a babbling Julia clinging to her hip. When she got close enough, she handed the baby to Jess. "She needs changing. And you need practice."

"Right this minute?"

"Yes, right this minute," Rachel said, grinning. "Her diaper bag's on my bed. And don't give me that look—it's not rocket science. Remove dirty diaper, clean little butt, put on clean diaper. Go on," she said, gently pushing Jess toward the door.

"If I'm not back in five minutes," he said, "send out the search-and-rescue dudes."

When Jess was gone, Rachel sat beside Thea, linking her hands through Thea's arm. "Feel better now? And don't say you weren't worried about me, because I know you were."

"It might be a tad soon to put that in past tense, honey."

A beat or two passed before the teenager said, "You know, what most people don't get is that Jess is my best friend. Believe it or not, we haven't been going at it like prairie dogs. That's only a real small part of what we have. Okay," she said, smiling and blushing, "maybe not *that* small a part. But still, it's not everything."

Steady brown eyes turned to hers. "And that's why I feel sure about this," she said, holding up her left hand with its shiny new gold band, before claiming Thea's arm again and laying her head on her shoulder. "I know this is gonna sound like a tacky greeting card, but...when Jess looks at me, I see forever—"

"O-kay," Jess said from the doorway. "*That* was probably the grossest moment of my life, but here you go." He handed the baby back to Rachel. "One clean kid. Can we eat now?"

Standing, Rachel laughed. "Sure thing. You coming?" she asked Thea, who shook her head.

"I don't dare show my face at the food table again while Ozzie's there. You two go on."

Who knew? Thea thought as they walked away, hands in each other's back pockets, Julia secure in Rach's other arm. Maybe they *would* beat the odds. Maybe, she thought as she walked into the wrecked, empty kitchen, one day they'd be one of those couples with their seventy-fifth wedding anniversary picture in the newspaper.

The room was dead quiet, save for the hum of the refrigerator. *Naptime,* she thought as the silence enveloped her, leading her farther into the house in search of a comfy sofa. Surely nobody would miss her for ten minutes....

And she knew just the sofa, she thought with a yawn, in a small, mostly unused den tucked on the other side of the house, a tribute to what passed for cutting-edge in 1968, when Maria Morales—dead for twenty years, at least—had last decorated it.

Unfortunately, somebody had already beaten her to it.

Like a bull asleep in a rose garden, Johnny lay sprawled on the faded chintz cushions, one booted foot propped on the sofa's far arm, the other still on the floor. Spread out on the marble-topped coffee table beside him were at least three photo albums, all open; it looked like he'd sat to have a look and keeled over. Muscled arm covering his eyes, he snored softly, a big old lump of testosterone on estrogen overload, and a lump of another sort rose in Thea's throat, at everything he'd been through this past week. Month. Hell, his entire life.

She started to leave, only to jump when a softly grunted

"Thea?" made her turn around again. Looking more than a little sheepish, Johnny had pulled himself upright again, yawning and combing one hand through his thick hair, and Itty-Bit nudged her, soft as a kitten's cautious poke, jostling loose all those wretched bonding hormones, and Thea once more found herself torn between wanting to wrap Johnny up tight and never letting go, and wanting to run as far as she could in the other direction and never look back.

Instead, she stood right where she was and just said, "Hey."

Chapter Seven

Much as he would've preferred to play it safe—or dumb, whatever worked—Johnny couldn't ignore his kick-to-the-gut reaction when he'd awakened and had seen Thea standing there, all that ambivalence naked in her eyes, and realized how easy it would be to take advantage of that ambivalence, just to assuage the constant, ragged hole in his own gut.

Why couldn't anything—just one thing, he wasn't picky—be simple and straightforward anymore?

He yawned. "Guess I passed out."

"Promise I won't tell," she said, which made him smile. "You hiding?"

"Hell, yes. You?"

"I was looking to score a quick nap. Except looks like Papa Bear beat me to it. Where's your wife?"

"*Ex*-wife. And I have no idea. Not here, obviously." He frowned. "You okay?"

"I'm fine. Just pregnant. Eat, sleep, bitch, that's my life these days. What's all this?" she said, coming to sit down like everything was perfectly normal between them and she wasn't pregnant and she didn't smell so good he thought he'd lose his mind. And Kat's words came back to him, especially all that stuff about loneliness, making his thoughts stumble around in his head like a bunch of confused drunks.

Johnny sighed, picking up a loose photo of Rach when she was ten, grinning out at him from atop her first full-size mare, Rosie. "How can this little girl be married, Thea? Be *pregnant?*"

"Just a thought, but maybe because she's not a little girl anymore?"

He dropped the photo back into the album and slammed it shut. "God knows what possessed me to drag out these things. Like the present's not giving me enough trouble without digging through the past. And you've been avoiding me."

"Just trying not to add to your *troubles.*"

"And you know damn well I didn't mean it that way."

"Doesn't matter. In any case," Thea said, getting up and walking over to a bookcase chock-full of forty-year-old paperbacks he'd never gotten around to tossing, "I kinda figured you had your hands full marrying off your daughter and entertaining your houseguests and the like."

If she'd been a horse, he'd be seeing flattened ears and flared nostrils right about now. And again it struck him how tender she was inside. How easily she could be hurt…how easily he could hurt her.

Whether he meant to or not.

"Daughter's married," he said mildly, tamping down the irritation, "*houseguest* is leaving in the morning. So I'm all yours."

She turned. "Why are those words sending chills down my spine?"

Johnny stood, making sure he was steady on his pins before

walking toward her, his hands rammed in his front pockets. "Maybe because you're picking up on how pissed I am? How'm I supposed to keep an eye on you when you won't answer your phone?"

"Okay, ignoring for the moment that whole 'keeping an eye on me' thing…I've been here almost every day helping with the wedding. So I was obviously okay. *Am* obviously okay." She pulled out a book, blowing off the dust before flipping it over to read the back. "I know Naomi said to keep you in the loop, but I don't think she meant checking in every twenty minutes…. Can I borrow this?" In front of his eyes, a faded couple in the throes of ecstasy looked like they were about to fall right off the cover. Or at least out of their clothes.

"What? Uh, yeah, take it. And if you'd just marry me, checking in wouldn't be an issue, because you'd already be here."

"Honestly, Johnny…not this again—"

"Yes, this again. It makes me crazy, thinking everything I've worked my ass off for over the last twenty years is gonna be shot to hell."

"Because I won't marry you? Oh, come on," she said when his jaw clenched, "raising a kid without being married…it's no big deal anymore. Not to anybody whose opinion I'd give two cents for, at least. And in any case, why on earth should anybody judge you for *my* decision?"

When he angled away, groping unsuccessfully for an answer that would make sense to anybody except him, Thea touched his arm. "This is nobody's business but ours. And you still can't honestly expect me to believe you really *want* to get married again."

"What I want has nothing to do with it. It's all about the kid—"

"Who'll be *fine.*" She hauled in a breath. "I know I've

never said this in so many words, but I'm proud of you, Johnny. Proud of the way you *have* moved beyond your past. And you'd better believe I'm proud to be having your baby. But I can't marry you."

"Won't marry me, you mean."

"Same difference."

"Why?"

"Because of the look in your eyes right now, for one thing. My refusal's not breaking your heart, it's just ticking you off. And for another…because I'm proud of everything I've overcome, too. And that includes not settling for something I know—we both know—isn't right."

"Because I want to make this legal?"

"The baby will have your name, it can't get much more legal than that. But I can't live a lie. And that's what marrying you would be. A big, fat lie. I mean, get real—you want to put this baby through what Rach went through when you and Kat got divorced? Because I sure as hell don't."

"But it's different between you and me than it was with Kat."

"That's right. You were in love with *her.*"

Oddly, there wasn't nearly as much pain as resignation behind her words. Still, it was frustrating as hell, trying to explain something he hardly understood himself. "And that was my first mistake, Thea. Leading with my feelings instead of my head. I knew better than to make a decision based on what felt good at the time instead of what made sense. What was practical. Kat and I…we had nothing in common. Nothing. Except for one thing that burned out real fast. But you and me—"

"Are friends. I know. And you have no idea how much I value that. But it's not enough. Not for me."

Heat rushed up his neck. "So whatever happened to all those conversations we had about love being a crock? That it can't be trusted, because it never lasts?" He closed in on her, his chest tight. "Whatever happened to your *realistic* outlook on life?"

"That hasn't changed. Because it occurs to me that being in love and being practical aren't mutually exclusive concepts. I can't believe I'm about to say this, but even Rach and Jess seem to have figured *that* out." Her eyes glittered. "Falling in love isn't a mistake, Johnny. Long as you don't fall in love with the wrong person."

Now he heard the hurt, one caused equally by Thea's idiot scumbag ex and—however inadvertently—him. "And I'm definitely the wrong person."

"It would appear so."

His forehead knotted. "Thought you said you *didn't* love me."

A look of extreme chagrin crossed her features. "What I am, is close enough to feel the heat, but still far enough away not to get burned," she said, and he felt sick that he couldn't make this right.

"I can offer you, and this baby, so much—"

"You don't love me, Johnny. And that's a deal breaker."

"So much for not wanting—and I quote—'all that messy stuff' again."

"Apparently I was kidding myself," she said quietly.

He held her gaze for a long moment before saying, "I would never cheat on you, Thea. I'm not your ex."

Her mouth dropped open. "I never said you were! Keith was all about manipulation and power plays and confusing sexual conquests with real manhood." Twin creases dug into the space between her eyebrows. "But holding back's almost as bad as sharing the wealth with all and sundry. Hurt is hurt, bucko. If I want loyalty, I've got five mutts waiting for me at home."

"Dammit, Thea…I don't know what to say."

"What's there to say? It's not like there's some kind of checklist for why love happens. Or doesn't. And anyway, the whys are immaterial. You can't help being who you are. But I can't help who I am, either. Or wanting what I want. You know I'd never cut you out of our baby's life. But for my own sanity I've got to keep you out of mine. As least as much as possible— Oh!"

Her eyes dipped to her middle; Johnny followed suit, noticing that one of the flowers on her dress was twitching.

"That the baby?"

"I sure as hell hope so. Even Naomi said he or she's a strong little bugger—" On a soft gasp, Thea lifted her eyes when Johnny palmed the bulge, firm and warm underneath the fabric.

He immediately let go. "Sorry, I should've asked—"

"No, no, it's okay, you just surprised me, is all. Here." She moved his hand to the other side of her belly. "Feel that?"

"Yeah," he said, afraid to move, to think past the moment. Except then he said, "We should really start thinking about names," and her eyes shot to his a second time.

"What's the rush?" she said, pulling away. Johnny grabbed her hand, ducking slightly to meet her afraid-to-hope gaze, and his heart shuddered.

"You can't jinx this. I promise."

Her eyes watered. "How's about neither of us makes any promises that are out of our control to keep?"

"Honey—"

"And you know, I really am pretty worn-out. Think I'll go on back to my place and crash, if you don't mind."

Oh, Johnny minded, all right. A helluva lot more than he had any right to. Which made no sense whatsoever. "You're really gonna leave before they cut the cake?"

Her lips curved in a sad, tired smile. "Mind asking Ozzie to save me a piece?"

"Of course not," he said, feeling oddly left out. Or something. "How big a piece are we talking?"

"Big enough to be embarrassing if I was eating it in public." She walked away, only to turn when she reached the doorway. "I'll call. Every day. I swear. Okay?"

Okay? Johnny thought after she was gone. Nothing about any of this was even remotely okay. Because it scared him, that he might lose her. Lose what they'd had.

Which had been good. Damn good. Better than good, it had been great. So why the hell did she have to go and screw everything up?

And more important, why couldn't he just let it go? Let *her* go?

Because this isn't about you, bonehead, he thought as he went back outside, where he spotted Naomi sitting underneath one of the cottonwoods, her bright skirt spread out around her. Before he could avert his gaze, she waved him over. Knowing resistance was futile, he went, lowering himself beside her on the cool, hard ground.

Not looking at him, she took a sip of whatever was in her cup. "You and Thea have a fight?"

Johnny shook his head, then sighed. "We're on opposite sides of the fence about a lot of things, but we don't actually fight. It's…weird."

"Yes. I imagine it is."

"You saw her leave, I take it?"

"Mmm," the doctor said, the ice rattling in her cup when she tilted it back. Johnny looked at her, his forehead pulled tight.

"She seem okay?"

"I have no idea, I wasn't close enough."

Nodding, Johnny raised one knee, balancing his wrist on top. "The baby's really doing fine, right?"

"Sure is. Why?"

"Because when I suggested that maybe we start thinking about names…you should have seen the look on Thea's face."

"Already seen it," she said, and Johnny grimaced.

"It doesn't seem right, her not letting herself get excited about this. Yeah, I know there's all this crap between her and me, but the baby…" He released another breath. "Hell, by the time Kat was this far along—"

"Thea's not Kat, Johnny," the doctor said, her tone almost sharp. "When you've had as many disappointments in your life as she has, you learn not to let yourself think about the future—only now. The pregnancy is a reality," she said, more gently. "The baby's still a hope. And hope's a scary thing. All Thea's life, the people she should've been able to trust the most have all let her down. Every single one of them. Then to lose three babies on top of that…can you blame her for guarding her heart?"

She paused, then looked straight ahead. "Seems to me if anybody understands that," she said, "it'd be you. And no, I don't expect a response. Oh, look…they're getting ready to cut the cake."

Reluctantly, Johnny got to his feet, then helped Naomi to hers. "In other words, I have to prove she can count on me?" he said to all those dreadlocks as they started back toward the food table.

Smiling, the doctor glanced over her shoulder. "Smart man," she said.

"This is so boring," Rachel said, shoving the two maternity tops she'd been considering back on the rack before looking across the customerless aisle, her face lighting up. "Oooh, baby stuff! Come on!"

"Rach! Get back here!" Thea barked, like the girl had just vanished into the Forbidden Forest, even as, with a little squeal, Rachel plucked an eensy-weensey, frilled-to-death dress off the first rack she came to. "It's way too early for you to be buying baby things!"

"Oh, come on, Thea—what can it hurt to just look?" Holding the tiny dress aloft, she giggled. "Isn't this, like, the most precious thing you've ever seen in your life? And anyway, it's not too early for you."

"Yes, it is," Thea said, mentally la-la-la-ing the siren call from the acres of sweetness on the other side. "Now get back over here. I have to work the evening shift tonight so I haven't got all day."

"Party pooper."

"*Now,* Rachel."

Her mouth turned down at the corners, Rachel reluctantly rehung the little dress and trooped back, where, on a weary sigh, she pronounced the entire department lame. Unfortunately, as Thea glowered at yet another baggy top with some idiotic sentiment plastered across it, she was tempted to agree with her.

"Why not just live in sports bras and yoga pants all summer? Strut around with your belly out like a hot fertility goddess."

"Omigod, Jess would have a cow. Not to mention Dad."

"Yeah, I can see where he'd have issues with that."

"What about you?"

"I have no issues whatsoever with you strutting around like a fertility goddess."

"Nooo...why don't you buy something for yourself?"

"Don't need anything. Wanna check out that maternity store on the lower level?"

"Sure, whatever," Rach said, her eyes longingly grazing the sea of cuteness as they headed toward the concourse exit. "I can't wait to find out what we're having. Not that I care one way or the other, I just want to know." Her pace slowed when they passed through the makeup department. "How about you?" Rach said, poking through a collection of perfume testers. A saleswoman who clearly made generous use of her employee discount drifted into view. "You gonna find out or wait and be surprised?"

"Haven't decided yet."

"It's just so much easier to plan the baby's room if you know what it's gonna be." The teen picked out a tester and sprayed her wrist, only to make a disgusted face. "Ugh. I forgot. Perfume makes me sick. Nothing personal," she said to the deeply offended saleswoman. "I'm pregnant. So's she, with my baby brother or sister. Isn't that cool?"

Thea steered Rach away before she invited the woman to the birth. "How is the morning sickness, by the way?"

"A *lot* better. You were right. The trick is to never let myself get hungry. Which reminds me…food court?"

"Sure."

"So," Rachel said as they traipsed past miles of sparkling plate glass and pasty mannequins in bizarre getups, "do you know whether Dad wants a girl or a boy?"

"We haven't discussed it. Oh, look…shoes—"

"You're kidding? God, it's like all Jess and I talk about. Okay, that's an exaggeration, we talk about lots more than that, but we've already got names picked out and everything." She tugged Thea away from the Payless and toward the escalator. "But we're not telling anybody because, frankly, it's our kid, so it's our decision." Once on the escalator, she turned slightly and said, "Can you believe Jess and I have been married three weeks already?"

What Thea couldn't believe is that she'd spent two hours with the girl and hadn't strangled her yet. Dear heavenly days, all this conjugal bliss was wearing on a person.

"Have to admit, though," Rachel continued, oblivious, "once I got the house pulled together and stuff…well, I'm kinda going nuts with nothing to do. Got so bored yesterday I started working my way through my old calculus textbook."

"Now that's just wrong," Thea said as they bounced off the escalator, and Rachel grinned, and Thea sighed, banishing her Inner Grouch. "Not to be pushy," she said, the food court in their sights, "but maybe you should take some college courses over the summer. Just to keep your brain from atrophying."

"Yeah, that's what Jess said, too. So maybe I will."

After several minutes' deliberation, they decided Subway fare would induce the least amount of pregnant-mommy guilt; now, settled with their sandwiches and ice water at a table Thea wasn't sure she actually wanted to touch, Rachel chomped off the end of her grilled-chicken sub and looked over at Thea.

"So," she said around a full mouth. "Wanna talk about it?"

"Talk about what?"

"Why you were scared to go into the baby department?"

Thea's stomach lurched. "I wasn't—"

"Uh, yeah. You were. Totally. Geez, you acted like that little dress was a bomb or something."

Thea set her gnawed-on sub back onto its crackly paper wrapper, dispatched a piece of escaped tomato and said quietly, "I'm guessing your dad didn't tell you I have a history of miscarrying."

The girl went pale. "Omigod, Thea…no, he didn't. I'm so sorry. But…" Her brow creased. "You're, what? Halfway along now?"

"I know. And Naomi swears everything's fine, but…I've kinda gotten used to being cautious." She took another bite of her sandwich. "And frankly, I'm pretty comfortable here."

"No kidding," Rachel said, bringing Thea's head up.

"What's that supposed to mean?"

"Nothing, sorry," she said, flushing to her tricolored roots. "Really, forget it—"

"Rachel."

"Okay. I know you and Dad… It's totally none of my business, okay? But Jess and I, we've been going to these newlywed counseling sessions—"

"You're kidding."

"Hello? Child of divorced parents here. You better believe I'm gonna do everything in my power to make sure this sticks. *Any*way…the dude there really keeps driving home how staying together takes work, you know? About how you can't just give up when things get tough, and that the number one reason for couples breaking up isn't sex, or money, or work issues, but lack of *communication.*" With a pointed look, the girl took a sip of her water. Thea sighed.

Lord, if Johnny'd had any idea how close she'd been to giving in to those dark, pleading eyes at Rachel's wedding…how hollow her "victory" had felt when she walked out of that den with her pride intact but her libido whimpering, *Are you insane?* When he'd laid his hand on her belly…uh, boy. Zero to sixty in two seconds flat.

Damn man always had known what buttons to push. In more ways than one. And glory be, pregnancy had basically turned her into one gigantic button. Yeesh, those bonding hormones were wicked.

However. Probably not the kind of communication Rachel meant.

"First off," Thea said, "your father and I already broke up, so this is all moot. Second, we talk. I check in with your father every day—"

"That doesn't count."

"Does in my book. Rach, I'm not sure what you're getting at, but lack of communication isn't what broke me and your dad up. We communicate just fine. It's agreeing on things we have problems with."

"Then you keep talking until you do."

Wondering if she'd been this obnoxiously self-confident at eighteen, Thea said, "You know, you're right, this *is* none of your business—"

"Don't you get it? Dad's scared. As scared of letting you get too close as you are of looking at baby clothes."

After a second's dizziness, Thea lobbed back, "And you're forgetting a major point, here—your dad doesn't love me."

"He actually told you that?"

"Those very words."

"And you believed him?"

"Why would he lie?"

"You tell me. All I know is," Rachel said, leaning forward, "those months the two of you weren't together? Dad was a basket case. Not so's anybody could tell, except maybe Ozzie, and Dad tried his best to hide it, to pretend everything was fine, but I know it wasn't. He really, really missed you."

Her appetite gone, Thea wrapped up the rest of her sandwich, considered tossing it into the trash, stuffed it into her purse instead. "So he said."

"Then what's—?"

"Rach, honey…as far as I know, I was your Dad's first, um, girlfriend of any note since he divorced your mom—"

"This isn't about—" she lowered her voice "—sex. I'll stake my life on that," she said, and Thea wondered how it was that Rach was the only teenager on the planet who could talk about sex and her own father in the same sentence and not get totally squicked out. "It's about him being lonely. About wanting something that for whatever reason he feels he can't have."

"Because he wants it on his terms, dammit!"

"Oh, and you don't?"

Her face heating, Thea stared the girl down. "The whole time I was growing up, I watched my mother turn herself inside out to be there for a man who didn't really want her, believing with all her heart that making him happy would make her happy. Well, let me tell you how well that model works," she said, getting to her feet and taking off.

"Thea! Wait!"

She heard frantic rustling behind her—sandwich being wrapped up, no doubt—then footsteps until Rach caught up with her in front of the maternity clothing store. She caught Thea's arm and pulled her around, the genuine worry in her eyes stealing Thea's breath.

"Dad *needs* you," Rach said, tears cresting, and Thea thought, *Why does everybody keep* saying *this?* "He won't admit it, maybe even to himself, but he does. You know how you just said you were his first girlfriend since the divorce? Well, think about that. I mean, did it even occur to you how huge a step that was for him, especially considering there were *plenty* of other women angling to get close?"

Okay, fine, so Thea'd seen Johnny rebuff his fair share of grass widows over the years. Felt, too, the darts of jealousy—the *Why her?*s—flung in her direction when she and Johnny finally outed their relationship—

"Don't you see?" Rachel said. "You gave up too soon. You're scared, he's scared…so you're both miserable. God! That's so bogus!"

"And your father and I can't be together simply because you're looking for verification from *somewhere* in order to feel better about your own decisions!"

Flushing, the teen's mouth dropped open. "That is so not true!" she cried, even though it was patently obvious that it so was.

"Whatever," Thea said, taking a page from Rachel's own book. "The fact remains, *the man told me he couldn't love me.* He wants companionship—and you can make of that what you will—without emotional commitment. I don't. So sue me for not being a big fan of unrequited love."

"For not having the guts to fight for what you want, you mean."

They stared each other down for several seconds before Thea said quietly, "You know, little girl, you're seriously beginning to piss me off."

"That was the idea," she said, then stomped into the maternity store. Thea considered leaving her there, only to remember they'd brought Rachel's car.

God save me from the starry-eyed, Thea thought, following her morosely into the store.

By the time Rachel dropped off Thea at her place, things between them were back to normal. Sort of. Okay, she knew she'd crossed a line—it was like she'd been totally powerless to stop all this *stuff* from pouring out of her mouth. But God! People said *teenagers* were brainless!

Catching sight of her father working one of the new foals in the paddock nearest the mares' barn, she parked close by rather than driving on to the cabin. Dad turned, smiling a little, and she thought about Thea's saying that Rachel wanted Dad and her to get together so *she'd* feel better. Well, duh. She loved them both, she wanted to see them happy. Preferably with each other, since she was guessing that was the only way *happy* was gonna happen for either one.

"How was the shopping trip?" Dad called over as she approached the paddock.

"Boring." She folded her arms on top of the post-and-rail fence. "Thea said hi."

"I'll just bet she did."

Tamping down the urge to swat her own father, Rachel watched him talk softly to the filly, stroking her to get her used to human touch. Sturdy little thing, brown-and-white spotted, with big brown eyes and long lashes like something out of a Disney movie. Pretty.

"How come you never told me about her miscarriages?" At her father's frown, she added, "When I tried to go look at baby stuff, she totally freaked. Wouldn't even set foot in the department. A little later I asked her what was up with that, and she told me. Since it didn't seem like any big secret, I just wondered why you hadn't."

Dad patted the foal's flank. "Thea doesn't like people fretting over her."

"Looks to me like she does that enough on her own," Rachel said, and Dad smiled. "I take it there was more than one?"

"Three," Dad said after a moment.

"Cripes. No wonder she's Looney Tunes about it."

"Rach."

"You know what I mean." She swatted at a fly, then asked, "Are you looking forward to this baby?"

Another frown. "What kind of fool question is that?"

"One I didn't get a right answer to. Geez, don't knock me over with your enthusiasm."

"Honey, I've been through this before. I *know* what lies ahead," Dad said with a hard look in her direction. "So I'm hardly gonna go around with a dumb grin on my face. Especially considering the circumstances, which aren't exactly ideal." The filly scampered back to her mother, her tail flicking. Her father watched mama and baby for a moment, then said, "This thing between Thea and me…" His gaze swerved back to hers. "It's…weird."

"You say that like it's a bad thing," Rachel said, and her father snorted. "You still want to marry her?"

"I want to make a home for her and our baby, yeah. But she's got…conditions for that to happen—"

"Like you loving her."

"That would be it."

"Dad, please don't take this the wrong way, but you're an idiot."

"Wouldn't be the first time somebody's made that observation."

"Okay, this is just my take on it…" Rachel swiped her hair out of her face. "But I don't think Thea's coping as well on her own—about the baby, I mean—as she wants everybody to believe. I know she told you to stay away, and I understand why, but…" Her mouth flattened. "Maybe it wouldn't hurt to be a little more, I don't know…" She tilted her head. "Involved? Like, you know, you were with me?"

When she started back to the car, her father called her back.

"Was that you saying I did okay with you?"

"Duh," she said, yanking open her car door. She was still riled when she pounded into the cabin a few minutes later to see Jess sitting on the ugly-ass plaid sofa Ozzie'd left behind, his bare feet propped on the equally ugly-ass coffee table and her laptop open on his knees.

"What are you doing home?"

Like, totally impervious to her hormonal mood swings, Jess looked up, half smiling. "It was slow." He patted the space next to him. "Eli said next week should be crazy, though. You didn't buy anything?"

"No," Rachel said, stepping over his legs to drop beside him, her arms crossed. With his left arm, Jess circled her shoulders, pulled her close. He'd obviously just showered; she rubbed her cheek against his clean T-shirt, soaking in his smell. "Honest to God," she muttered, "between Thea and my father…are there two more stubborn, clueless people on the face of the freaking planet?"

"To save time," Jess said, tapping the computer's mouse

pad, "I'm just gonna assume I know what you're talking about. Oh, almost forgot—package came for us, over there. From your mom."

"Did you open it?" Rachel said, nearly doing in her shin on the edge of the coffee table when she shot up to pounce on the FedEx box. The *big* FedEx box.

"Nah, I figured I'd let you have the fun. What's in it?" he asked distractedly as she tore into the thing.

"Enough baby stuff for quadruplets? Holy cow…I think it's safe to say she's okay with being a grandma—"

"Day-um."

"What?"

"Wanna see what our kid looks like right now?"

Rachel clambered back over the table to plunk down again, squinting at the screen. She'd had her first sonogram, but who could tell anything from that? This was, like, three-dimensional and everything. "Oh, wow…it's got fingers and toes already?"

"Yeah. Crazy, huh? Hey…what's wrong?"

Tears clogging her throat, she shook her head, thinking about Thea losing her babies, suddenly afraid for her own. Jess looped his arm around her again, then said, "You've gotta stop getting so wound up about your dad and Thea—it's not good for you or the baby."

"Why do you think—"

"We've got enough on our own plates right now, trying to prove to everybody we're not gonna screw this up. I know you're worried about your dad, baby," he said softly, "but you know how it pisses you off, the way he's always trying to fix stuff? Well, neither can you. Whatever's going on between him and Thea, they're gonna have to work it out on their own. That's all I'm saying. So. You want burgers for dinner? I found this old grill in the shed out back, cleaned it up and it's good to go."

Her stomach rumbled for the eight thousandth time that day. "Burgers sound great. Just make sure mine's well done—rare's not good for the baby."

"You got it," Jess said, giving her a quick grin and a kiss before getting up to go out back, clearly expecting Rachel to snap out of it.

Did he have a lot to learn, or what?

Chapter Eight

"Yeah, yeah, yeah," Thea muttered over the dogs' thrilled-to-bits barking as she waded through the sea of panting fur to her door, fetchingly dressed for the ridiculously hot July day in a baggy tank top and drawstring shorts, shoes optional.

"Hey, Eli," she said, spotting Jesse's older brother when she opened the door. Same dimples, same pretty brown eyes, same smile, but ten years older, several inches taller and probably thirty pounds heavier. Big dude. The dogs went nuts. "You're early." Underneath a head of soft, light brown curls, he flashed a devastating smile, and Thea thought, *How is it you're still single?*

"I had a crapload of other deliveries to make today. You were first on the list."

"Oh, okay, let me help you—"

"Forget it, you shouldn't be hauling stuff in your condition. I'll be right back."

Shoving things around in her work area to make room for the wooden blanks she'd ordered, she pondered the wisdom of maybe getting the air conditioner fixed or replaced or something. Normally the ceiling fans did just fine—especially since it cooled off so much at night—but this heat gave new meaning to the expression "bun in the oven." In the past six months she'd gone from always sick to always hungry to always hot.

In more ways than one, she thought ruefully when Eli returned, two boxes of wooden cutouts balanced in his buff arms, the white cotton of his T-shirt hugging muscles worthy of a porn star. Not that she was thinking of Jesse's brother in those terms—please, she'd sat for him when he was an obnoxious eight-year-old whose fave pastime was launching water balloons at unsuspecting babysitters—but those rippling muscles were definitely getting her juices going.

Aaaand the too-pregnant-to-boogie phase could kick in anytime now. Please *God,* let it kick in.

She'd only seen Johnny once since the Shopping Trip from Hell, when he'd accompanied her to her last appointment. He hadn't exactly been chatty, opting instead for silent, sullen mode. Lots of long, thoughtful, unnerving stares, like he was trying to figure something out. Her, most likely. And still, the sexual buzzing had damn near deafened her. Even Naomi'd noticed. At least, Thea assumed that's what prompted the doctor's completely unsolicited—and, thank God, private—assurance that Thea was good to go for sex, should the opportunity, um, arise.

And yes, she'd actually said that with a straight face.

"I'm amazed you can still find time to make these for me," Thea said as she went to get her purse from the kitchen, shaking off hormones right and left along the way. "You must be pretty busy, what with your furniture business taking off and all."

Squatting in a mass of wriggling dogs, Eli grinned up at her, all charm and devilment and suddenly reminding her way too much of her ex—in the early days, at least, when she still liked him—and she decided he needed a sign that said *Not ripe yet, put it back.* "Did Jess tell you? I got accepted into two major art shows in Albuquerque in the fall."

She handed him his check. "No, I haven't seen Jess and Rach all that much." And yes, that made her a great big chicken. Cluck, cluck. But there was only so much *But why can't you two work it out?* whining a body could take. "So, go, you!" she said, giving Eli a fist bump, which—she was grateful to note—produced no buzzing, humming, tingling or any other even remotely sexual reaction. Apparently pregnancy hadn't turned her into a nympho after all. Good to know. "How's Jess doing, by the way?"

Eli stood, shaking off dogs. "Driving me nuts, actually. He's got all these ideas for promoting my work, thinks I should get a Web site, start selling on the Internet. Man, marriage has turned him into one scary dude." He checked his watch. "So," he said, arms crossed, head bobbing. Eyes lingering too long on baby bump. "How's it going?"

Thea nearly choked. "Oh, hell, Eli—*please* don't tell me you're one of those men with a thing for pregnant women."

"What?" The poor dude flushed a deep red. "*No!* Geez, Thea, it would be like hitting on my mother or something. What makes you say that?"

"Because you're still here, making small talk, when you said you had a whole bunch of deliveries to make—" Her mouth fell open. "Excuse me? Your *mother?*" He shrugged, chuckling, cute as all hell as he checked his watch. Again. "And why do you keep looking at your watch?"

At that precise moment, another vehicle pulled up outside and Eli visibly relaxed. "Got a surprise for you," he said, striding to the open door. "Yeah, man," he said to whoever was on the other side. "It's in the truck. Came out real nice, too."

What now? Thea thought as she followed, her eyebrows popping up when she saw Johnny standing at the open tailgate of Eli's pickup, hands on hips, expression serious, watching Eli carefully lift out what sure as heck looked like…

A cradle.

"Oh my God," she whispered, right before the world went black.

"Get a damp cloth or something!" Johnny barked at Eli as Thea crumpled in his arms, Johnny's heart went into overdrive and his back nearly went out. Damn, how much weight had she gained? "Thea…honey? You with me? Thea?"

Her eyes popped open; she struggled to sit up, fending off slurping tongues—none of them human—and a dripping-wet washcloth. "Geez, y'all—lighten up!" She blinked at Johnny. "How long was I out?"

"About thirty seconds."

"Oh, well, then." Her eyes traveled to the cradle. "Um…what's that?"

"Something to put the baby in once it's on the outside?" he said, plowing ahead when her head started to wag. "Eli showed me some plans, and this one…" He glanced over his shoulder at the cradle, then back at the *Oh, hell* look on her face. "I don't know, it just looked like you. Like something you'd like, I mean."

She clamped her hands over her mouth, quietly keening.

"I told you you should've gone with that other one," Eli said, and Thea let out a sputtery laugh.

"No, n-no, it's just…"

Her mouth pulled flat, tears swelling over her lower lids. These past weeks Johnny'd about sprained his brain trying to figure out how to make all the pieces fit. But as much as he'd tried to be sensitive to Thea's fears at the beginning, her continued reluctance to discuss names or find out the baby's sex or fix up a nursery, even in this wretched place…

Wasn't right, her still having so many doubts, not being able to enjoy the very thing she'd waited so long for. So, yeah, he'd known he was taking a risk, springing this on her. But as aggravating as his daughter was, hoping for magic where it wasn't going to happen, he had to admit that she—and Naomi, because, okay, he'd begun to see a pattern here—had a point: that maybe if he showed Thea how committed he was to their kid, she'd begin to let go of at least some of the fear. It wasn't much—wasn't everything she needed and wanted from him—but it was something.

Johnny took her rough little hand, and her eyes shot to his, full of surprise and immediate sexual awareness, and he gritted his teeth against his reaction and said, "Honey, you're six months pregnant. I think it's safe to say it's gonna stick. Naomi said you're good, the baby's good—"

"And things happen," she whispered, shivering in a dry, gritty breeze that smelled of petunias and marigolds and the ghosts of cheap gasoline; worn-out from all the excitement, her dogs had turned into so many furry, inert yard ornaments, collapsed in assorted splotches of shade.

"Yeah, well, what happened was, you got pregnant. And you're gonna have a baby. *This* baby. In three months, give or take. And you need to start getting ready for it. Have you even told your mother yet?"

"No," she breathed out as Eli backed away, mumbling something about really needing to get going.

"Oh," Thea said, like she'd forgotten he was still there. She stood, opening her arms to give him a hug. "The cradle really is beautiful, thanks," she said, giving him a peck on the cheek.

Johnny stood, as well, his gut clenching, that Eli could smell that special smell that rose up off Thea's neck when she was warm. Not until Eli's truck was long gone, however, did she turn back around, her gaze soft on his.

"So what's this all about?"

There was a $64,000 question for you.

She'd pulled her short hair back into a strange, shaggy little ponytail. Only most of it didn't quite reach the elastic band, leaving all these wispy little ends dangling around her face. Johnny slowly closed the short distance between them to brush a strand off her temple, a simple gesture that worked something lose he'd thought taped up good and tight. Not completely, just enough that he'd have to keep an eye on it.

"What this is about," he said to puzzled eyes as sweat trickled down his back, "is me realizing that the one flaw in staying out of your way is that we're still supposed to be friends. And friends don't put each other through hell just because one of 'em happens to be pregnant."

A laugh burbled through her nose. "You are too much," she said, shaking her head, her expression a mix of amused and wary. Her arms folded over her round belly. "You gonna stop pestering me to marry you?"

"Oh, the offer's still on the table. But I'm not gonna bug you about it anymore, no."

"Truly?"

"Cross my heart," he said, doing just that.

"But you still think I'm a blamed fool."

Chuckling, Johnny pulled Thea into his arms, copping a smell. Even if it was just a "friendly" hug. "What I think," he murmured into her hair, "is that you might want to rethink your game plan pretty soon or you're gonna have a naked baby with no place to sleep."

She wriggled against his chest enough to look at the cradle, still outside her front door. "Looks like you got the place to sleep part covered."

"For a few months, at least," he said, letting go. Because friendly hugs had definite time limits. "Babies don't stay little very long. But actually..." He ducked his head slightly, peering at her from underneath his hat brim. "Last time I was at Wal-Mart, I might've bought a couple things." Another idea he'd gotten from Rachel, even if inadvertently, after watching her ooh and ahh over all the baby stuff Kat had sent. "You know, to tide us over."

At the *us,* Thea's gaze snapped to his. "I see."

"Would you like to? Got it all right in the truck."

Her eyes widened, stirring with the very beginnings of interest. "Oh, yeah?"

"Of course, if you don't—"

"Bring it here," she said, wheeling around to his truck, quivering like a kid at Christmas. When he didn't move right away, she faced him again, all impatience. "Well, what are you waiting for?" She made a bring-it-on gesture with her hands. "Mama wants to see her presents."

"They're not for you, they're for the *baby,*" Johnny said, moving past her on his way to the truck, her exasperated "What*ever*" behind him making him grin.

Well, hell—you don't suppose he'd finally done something *right?*

"Hate to tell you," Thea said, sitting cross-legged on her bed, her emotions bouncing around like kindergartners at recess, "but this isn't just 'a couple of things.'"

"Okay, so I might've gotten carried away."

"Ya think?" She dumped out the fourth crammed-to-the-gills bag onto the jewel-toned Log Cabin quilt Mama'd made for her when she got married, fussing at the dogs for the twentieth time to go away, this wasn't for them. And with each bag, each tiny sleeper and package of booties, each brightly colored baby toy or bib with a funny saying on it, the little critter growing inside her became less The Thing That Made Her Constantly Pee and more a real little person who'd soon wear or play with or listen to all this stuff.

"Ohhhh..." She scooped up the adorable, floppy-eared stuffed puppy attached to a "lovey," satin on one side, soft plush on the other, hugging it to her own cheek. J.D. got up on the bed and barked, jealous. Thea shoved him off again. "You're gonna make me cry," she said, sniffing. To Johnny, not the dog.

"Again?" Johnny said, and Thea looked over at him, lounging across the head of the bed with his head propped in his palm, looking so damn tickled with himself, and she thought, *You're not helping matters any.* Because with every bag and bootie and bib, those bonding hormones shrieked a little louder, a little longer, and she lost her battle a little more, not to fall all the way in love with him.

"Again," she said, reaching across him to grab a tissue off the nightstand to blow her nose. Only, forgetting her boobs took up more space than usual, one nipple grazed his shoulder and she nearly popped out of her skin.

And that was with three layers of clothing between them. Not to mention no purposeful intent.

Then she caught his gaze, dark and most definitely purposeful, and she wondered, first, how on earth the man could be turned on with her looking such a sight, and second, what was that about their being friends again?

Of course, then Thea remembered that Johnny's being a man pretty much canceled out both those things, what with pheromones not giving a rat's hiney about friendship. Basically, what they had here was the potential for history to repeat itself.

"So I done good?" Johnny said as she straightened again, pretending everything was normal, even as something in his voice pierced straight through the hormonal haze and made her meet his eyes, which she knew was a seriously bad idea but whatchagonna do?

And there, behind the crooked, cocky grin, the relaxed posture, lurked a vulnerability that shook her to her core. Not that she hadn't had glimpses before, slight though they might have been. But those had been like tricks of the light, maybe you saw something and maybe you didn't. This time, however, it was like somebody'd flung open a door and shined a light on the nameless creature, naked and quivering and frightened, huddled in the corner of Johnny's soul.

Except then something shifted in Johnny's eyes and the door slammed shut again, as if to say *Just your imagination, honey, don't give it another thought.*

But it wasn't her imagination, she'd definitely seen something. And she knew she'd never rest until she ferreted it out to get a better look. Someday, though. Not now.

"You done real good," she said, smiling, picking up a tiny sleeper with yellow bunnies all over it and stretching it over her belly. The baby stirred, content. Like she'd once been, before she'd gone and done the deed with Johnny Griego. "You actually picked all this out by yourself?"

"I actually did. Did it the first time, too. With Rach."

Thea gave Johnny a dumbfounded look, but he was too busy prying a rubber ducky out of Bugly's mouth to notice. "*You* bought all her baby things?"

"Well, Kat got a buttload of stuff at her shower—which I imagine you will, too," he said, and Thea realized she'd never even considered that possibility, even though she was going to Winnie's in a couple of weeks, "but you know how it is, people always give you a dozen of the same thing— Let *go,* dog! *Thank* you." He checked the dog-slimed ducky for puncture marks, then swiped it across his jeans. "And Kat kind of had a rough time for a few weeks afterward, so the gap-filling fell to me."

The image of Mr. Macho here picking out sleepers and what-all…mind-boggling. Cute as hell, but mind-boggling. Then Thea frowned at him. "Kat had a hard time?"

"Bad case of the baby blues. Took me nearly a week before I realized how serious it was." He paused. "Took me a lot longer'n that to get over thinking I was somehow to blame."

"You're not serious."

"Doesn't matter now," he said. "What matters now—" he got up, surveying the space "—is figuring out where you're gonna put this kid once…it's born."

Because while the cradle worked just fine right beside the bed, Thea had to admit she had no earthly idea where she'd put a crib.

"The baby's not an *it,*" she said, suddenly annoyed, even though that was stupid since she'd been the one refusing to find out whether they were having a boy or a girl.

Not looking at her, Johnny said, very quietly, "Isn't the suspense killing you?"

Several beats passed before the penny dropped. "Omigod—you know, don't you?"

He turned, the corners of his mouth lifted. "I know you told Naomi you didn't want to find out, so she made me swear on the Bible and every relative's grave dating back to the Civil War not to say anything unless you asked, but yeah. I've known since your last appointment. And by the way…this isn't *a* baby, or *the* baby. It's *our* baby. Now would you like to know if we're having a son or a daughter?"

Slowly, Thea rose from the bed and walked over to him,

almost hating him for knowing. Almost. "And if I say I still don't?"

Evil grin time. "I've kept it to myself this long, won't kill me to keep my mouth shut for another three months." His grin widened. "Might kill you, though."

"Creep."

He winked at her. "Want a hint?"

"No." She shut her eyes, her heart hammering in her chest. "Yes," she whispered, and a second later Johnny'd taken her by the arms and turned her back to the bed.

"If you notice," he said softly, his breath caressing her ear, "everything's gender-neutral. Except one thing, which only came in two colors. Frankly, I was surprised you didn't pick up on it the minute you saw it."

At that, her gaze zeroed in on the puppy-lovey, which was a solid, perfect, cloudless sky…blue.

"We're having a little boy?" she whispered.

She heard Johnny pull something out of his shirt pocket; a second later, the sonogram picture floated in front of her eyes, blurred though they were. A tiny circle had been drawn somewhere in the middle, with an arrow pointing to the crucial element.

Boy parts, it said.

On a sob, Thea turned into Johnny's rock-solid chest, letting the tears come while the dogs circled them, panting and confused, as she wondered how she could feel so safe and apprehensive at the same time. Could she really do this? Accept the friendship she'd missed so much, needed more than she wanted to admit, even as her heart and mind and body teetered on the brink of…well, disaster, if she was being truthful?

Then Johnny said, gently rubbing her back, "If you want, I'll even go with you when you tell your mother," which was exactly the right thing for him to say, even if Thea hadn't known it before that very moment, and she nodded, teetering a little more.

Took Johnny another two weeks to convince Thea they needed to drive up to Durango to see her mother before she got too uncomfortable to sit for long periods. And although she'd seemed chipper enough this morning when they started out, the minute they'd crossed the Colorado border her expression had changed as dramatically as the sudden shift from red rock mesas to dense conifer forests.

"Your mother does know you're coming, right?"

"Of course," she breathed out, allowing him a small smile. "She still doesn't know why, though."

"I'm guessing she'll figure it out pretty fast."

Thea blew a soft laugh through her nose. "Part of me thinks she'll understand why I kept it to myself, but…" She paused. "She never did quite forgive me for 'giving up'—" she made quotes in the air "—on Keith. No surprise there, I suppose."

Johnny already knew that her father's cycle of infidelity/abandonment/begging her mother to take him back had frayed her heart, little by little, until he'd finally walked out for good when Thea was a teenager. Thea couldn't fathom why her mother'd tolerated her father's behavior for so long; in her turn, Sheila Benedict had never been able to understand Thea's issues with her mother's loyalty, a sticking point that had kept mother and daughter at odds for the last twenty years.

"In any case, this baby deserves to know his only grandparent," Johnny said, getting a sighed, "Yeah, I know," in response.

And wasn't it beyond ironic, Johnny's trying to patch things up between Thea and her mother, considering his own views about rooting around in the past?

One thing about Kat: she'd never seemed particularly interested in digging below Johnny's surface, despite her considerable journalistic skills at uncovering the truth. Which had been just fine and dandy with him. Pointless, is what it was, rummaging around in a bunch of bad memories, like faded photographs of events you'd just as soon forget. So he'd been relieved when Thea hadn't seemed real big on that whole soul-searching thing, either. Not that their personal history was off-limits or anything—for the most part—long as they were talking about stuff that was, as they say, a matter of public record.

Something had shifted, though, that afternoon he'd brought her the cradle. More than once she'd looked at him like she could see straight through him, like the wall hiding all the crap he didn't want to think about anymore had begun to crumble. Not a lot, just enough to be worrisome. Because before that, Johnny'd had no doubts about his ability to fulfill his obligations and still remain impervious to everything that was Thea. Now, however…

Now, crumbling walls or not, he was in up to his eyeballs.

What was it they said? Something about no good deed going unpunished?

Thea's cell phone rang, disrupting his thoughts. From her response, he gathered the call had something to do with her taking her crafts to the local flea market the next day. "Problem?" he asked after she slipped her phone back into her purse.

"What? Oh. Sort of. The gal I was gonna share the flea market booth with can't make it, on account of her son and his wife coming into town unexpectedly."

"You certainly can't do it by yourself," Johnny said, and Thea chuckled.

"For once I have to agree with you. Can't leave everything unattended while I pay nineteen visits to the Porta-Potty. So

I guess I'll have to skip it this weekend… Oh! That's the turnoff to my mother's development right up ahead."

A minute later, they drove into a condominium complex of cookie-cutter, steeply roofed, Tudor-style town houses nestled among green lawns dotted with clumps of skinny aspens and adolescent evergreens. Thea'd been here once before, she'd said, when her mother had remarried a few years back and moved in with her new husband.

"Make a right here, it's the fourth one in."

They pulled in alongside a sparkling-clean, upscale SUV hybrid; Johnny glanced over to see Thea clutching her purse, white-knuckled. "It'll be okay, honey," he said, and she said, "Uh-huh," not moving, so he got out and went around to pry her loose; otherwise, they'd be sitting here all day. Her feet had no sooner touched asphalt when he heard a shrieked "Eddie! They're here!" behind him.

He supposed he'd seen Sheila Benedict before, when Thea and her mother had still both lived in Tierra Rosa, but he had no recollection of the dainty blonde in a starchy-looking, fitted orange blouse and knee-length white pants now bearing down on them with open arms. Not at all what he'd expected, although he couldn't have told you what that had been. But whoever she was, the instant she saw Thea she pressed her hands over her heart, eyes a little greener than Thea's immediately swimming with tears.

"Oh my God, honey. Omigod, omigod, omigod." With each "omigod," she came closer, until she'd swallowed up her very pregnant daughter in a huge, laughing hug, her face buried in Thea's hair, hanging on until, very slowly, Thea's arms tightened around her, too.

Chapter Nine

"Let's you and I go inside and give the women some time alone," said an avuncular voice behind Johnny. Startled, he turned, his gaze bumping into smiling blue eyes set in a long, thin face underneath a gray, military-issue buzz cut.

"Ed Avery," the older man said, extending his hand, then clapping Johnny's shoulder with the other. The grip was firm, belying the slack-muscled arm coming out of the loose-fitting golf shirt. "And you must be Johnny."

"Uh, yeah. Sorry—"

"No need to apologize." The eyes crinkling, Ed started up the short flight of stairs to the front door. "You may as well come on, they'll catch up when they're ready. I'm not much of a drinker, but we did get some beer in, just in case."

Forcing his gaze away from Thea and her mother—who'd moved on from hugging to wiping tears off each other's faces—Johnny reluctantly followed, his eyes bugging out when he walked into the cool, quiet living room.

It was a damned one-person craft fair, sporting quilts on every wall and crocheted throws on every chair and painted geegaws and whatchamacallits everywhere else—

"Sheila's sure talented, isn't she?" Ed said, proud. "Always got some project or other going—you should see our spare bedroom." He laughed. "Or not. Last time I went in there it took me a week to find my way out again. I hear Thea's got a gift, too."

Johnny swallowed his smile. "I can certainly see where she gets her…inspiration."

"Yeah, Sheila's inspiring, all right," the older man said with a quiet laugh. "But you know, first time I complimented her on one of her pieces, she got all teary on me. Finally admitted her ex did nothing but criticize her about her hobby, told her it was stupid. A waste of time."

Johnny's face warmed. "That's terrible."

"To say the least. You ask me, the bastard was just jealous of anything that took time away from Sheila taking care of him. When he bothered to remember he had a wife, that is. So she learned to keep her supplies and what-all at a friend's house, sneaking in her projects when he wasn't around. Only thing that kept her sane, she said. Her, and Thea."

"Thea?"

"Oh, yeah. Thea apparently didn't go in much for the sewing and stuff, but she loved painting from the time she was little. The brighter the colors, the more she liked 'em. Said she liked making 'her own rainbows,' according to Sheila." He paused. "It means the world to her, Thea's coming up to see her like this. Of course, she didn't know about the baby, that's just icing on the cake. And if that baby's the means of fixing whatever was broke between them, so much the better. Now. Let's get you that beer…."

* * *

Thea stood by the kitchen door, watching Mama zip back and forth in the gleaming, efficient little kitchen and trying to sort out the odd combination of awkwardness and familiarity at being with her mother again after so many years, wondering why this time seemed different somehow. "What can I do to help?"

"Absolutely nothing," her mother said, pulling tubs of deli coleslaw and potato salad out of the side-by-side stainless-steel fridge, "except sit *down,* for heaven's sake, and put your feet up. Your ankles look puffy."

"They are not." Her mother glared at her. "Okay, maybe a little." So she sat, propping her sandaled feet on an extra kitchen chair, trying not to listen to Johnny's and Ed's voices coming in through the open patio door from the deck. It was all just a little too serenely surreal for her taste, but her mother certainly seemed happy enough. Genuinely happy, as opposed to the grin-and-bear-it faux cheer of Thea's childhood.

The thing was, she loved her mother. Always had. Maybe she'd thought the woman a few bricks shy of a load for her blind devotion to a man who didn't deserve it, but Thea couldn't in all honesty say she'd ever felt neglected, or second in her mother's affections. If anything, Mama had bent over backward to give Thea as normal and happy a childhood as possible, given the circumstances. And despite how much her own heart must have been breaking. In fact, there'd been a lot more good times when it'd just been the two of them than when her father'd been in the picture…a realization that made her cringe at her own blindness and self-involvement.

"Ed seems like a real good guy," she said softly. "I like him."

Mama turned around, clearly pleased. "You really do?"

"I really do."

Her mother reached up into a cupboard for a couple of serving bowls. "Not that I need your approval."

"God, no," Thea said, then pushed out, "I'm so sorry, Mama."

This time, the look included a creased brow. "For what?"

"You know what."

After a moment, Mama grabbed a spoon from the drawer in front of her, dumped the coleslaw into one of the bowls. "It's okay, baby. I'm just glad you're here now."

"So am I," Thea said, and her mother nodded.

Only to twist around again, pointing at her with the spoon. "Although I cannot *believe* you waited this long to tell me about the baby!"

"I…didn't want to get your hopes up. Again."

"Didn't want to get *your* hopes up again, you mean," she said gently.

"That, too."

Her mother went back to carefully smushing the coleslaw into a nice, neat mound. "Have to say, Johnny's nothing like I remember. Not that I knew him all that well, really, but I have this image of him glowering all the time, like he was mad at the world. Before he started working up at the ranch, anyway. He seemed to settle down some after that. And now you say he *owns* it?"

"Has for years. Andy Morales left it to him." Thea cupped her belly, watching it ripple underneath her loose, sleeveless top. "I admire your restraint."

"About?"

"Me and Johnny not getting married."

Her mother moved on to gouging the potato salad out of its plastic deli tub. "You're a grown woman, Anthea." The salad plopped into the bowl. "How you live your life is your concern. Besides, it's no big deal these days, having kids without being married. It's just…"

And heeere it comes, Thea thought as her mother banged the spoon into the bowl and grabbed a paper towel to wipe her fingers. Then she sat at the table, the crumpled towel still clutched in her hand. "Honey…after what you went through with that boneheaded ex of yours? Not to mention how your daddy treated the two of us? I don't blame you one bit for being gun-shy about getting married again."

"What—"

"But just from the little I've seen you two together? I can tell Johnny's no more like Keith, or your daddy, than Ed is. Hard as it may be to believe, not all men are dirtwads."

"But…all those years you let Daddy tramp all over you—"

"I know, I know…" Mama got up, going to the counter to pull a package of jumbo hamburger buns out of a plastic grocery bag. "Right or wrong, I was raised to believe that long-suffering just came with the territory, like knowing how to cook and iron and fake orgasms."

Thea choked on her laugh. "I can't believe you just said that!"

"Yeah, well, I can't believe I bought into that crock as long as I did, either, that a woman's role in life was to be patient and forgiving, because men couldn't help their 'true natures.'" This, accompanied by a shudder.

"I'm taking it you didn't get the notice going around in the '60s informing women they didn't have to put up with that crap?"

"That notice didn't reach a lot of us living in the boonies. Apparently still hasn't. But my point is, I really believed I could love your father into changing, that eventually he'd realize I was the one who was always there for him, no matter what." Pain sharpened her gaze. "What I didn't realize is what a horrible, *horrible* example I was setting for you. Not until you married a man exactly like your father did it finally hit me how badly I'd failed you."

"Why on earth didn't you say anything?" Thea said, dumbfounded.

"Knowing I'd failed was one thing. Admitting it was something else."

"You didn't fail me, Mama—"

"Yes, I did. I know it, you know it, no sense in pretending otherwise. My only solace is that at least you caught on a helluva lot faster than I did. Once you realized Keith was cheating on you, what's that saying? His ass was grass?"

When Thea's laughter subsided, she said, "Even so, it took a while to find the courage to kick that ass to the curb. Because you're right, it's hard to admit we've failed. Damn hard—"

"But we didn't fail, baby! Not about that, anyway," Mama added, reddening. "They did! It wasn't our fault!"

Thea smirked. "We picked 'em, didn't we?"

"Please. I was eighteen when I ran away with your father. You were—what?—twenty when you married Keith? What the hell did we know then?"

"And maybe age has nothing to do with it," Thea said, thinking of Rachel. Irritatingly optimistic as the girl might be, she wasn't blind. Somehow Thea suspected one indiscretion on Jesse's part and Rach would kick *his* butt to the curb and not look back.

"Even so," Mama said, "while I know I let you down by not being a better example—and you'd better believe no man will ever treat me again the way your daddy did—I've also learned there're good men out there. Ed's one of 'em." With a slight smile, she added, "And I'm guessing Johnny is, too."

"Well, yes, he is, but—"

"Every time your daddy'd leave…omigod, it broke my heart, seeing how sad you were. Then he'd come back, and your little face would light up—" she leaned over to palm Thea's cheek "—and I'd think, *See, you're doing the right thing.* Only then he'd leave, again, and you'd be devastated—again..." A tear slipped down her cheek. "I'm so, so sorry, baby."

Then she straightened, her light coral lipstick disappearing when she pressed her lips together. "But only because I wasted all those years loving the wrong person. My love was wasted on your daddy, because he didn't need me. Or appreciate me. And heaven knows he didn't *deserve* me." Mama's head swiveled toward the sound of the men's laughter, then back to Thea. "The good ones, though," she said with a gentle smile, "they are worth fighting for."

Thea opened her mouth, except the baby poked her in the ribs, making her jump. Her mother sucked in a little breath.

"Can I feel?"

"Sure." Thea took Mama's hand to lay it over the kicking, only to laugh when her mother hunched over to press her ear against Thea's stomach. "That's a real soccer player you got in there," she said. "Y'all picked out a name yet?"

"Working on it," Thea said, as Mama sat up again. Then, frowning at her tummy as she rubbed it, she asked softly, "How do you fight for somebody who'll give you everything but his heart?"

Her mother laid her hand over hers, making Thea look into her eyes. "By giving him all of yours," she whispered.

Not gonna happen, Thea thought.

No. Damn. Way.

"Hey, sleepyhead—we're back."

At Johnny's light touch on her wrist, Thea shook herself out of her doze. Okay, not so much *doze* as *out cold.* Yeesh. She could only hope the baby would fall asleep as easily as she did these days.

He'd put the windows down, letting in the cool, woodsy breeze. And a chorus of yips and barks from the gang out back. Yawning so hard she half expected to see trees bow in her direction, Thea blinked through the windshield at the crazy, sunset-drenched jungle of painted flowers and vines on the walls of her "house." Ordinarily a sight to make her heart sing. Tonight, though…not so much.

"Wow," Johnny said beside her, leaning hard on the steering wheel and gazing up at the display like a kid seeing Disneyland for the first time. "In this light, it's really something. Like…magic."

And maybe she wasn't really awake after all. "I know men aren't generally known for their powers of observation, but you've been out here I don't know how many times since I painted that wall. And you're just now noticing?"

"Oh, I noticed." He sat back, adjusting his hat on his head. "What I hadn't done before was appreciate it."

"Appreciate it?"

"Yeah," he said, his gaze glancing off hers before he turned away again. "You know, if it ever seemed like I was putting down what you do, I apologize. Where I got off thinking it was okay to criticize something that obviously gives you so much pleasure—"

"Okay, Johnny. You can quit right now, because for one thing you're scaring me. And for another, you don't have to apologize for anything, it's not like I ever took it seriously."

"Good to know," he said, with that lopsided smile that made her go all syrupy inside. Then he looked at her again, the smile gone. "It's just that Ed told me how your daddy used to give your mama grief about her crafts, so…" He shrugged.

"Ah. I see." She looked away, the backs of her eyes burning. "I swear, Johnny, I've never taken offense."

"Never?"

"Not once," she said, laughing away the sting before meeting his contrite gaze. "For heaven's sake, I only do this stuff for fun, and to make a few extra bucks, but it's not like I ever pretended to be a real artist. Aidan's an artist, I'm just a waitress who likes to play with pretty colors from time to time. And anyway, there's a world of difference between you teasing me about my silly coyotes and my father's control issues. He was downright mean. You couldn't be mean if your life depended on it."

Their gazes wrestled for several seconds before, totally out of the blue, he leaned over and kissed her. Not hard and not long, but sometimes a kiss isn't *just* a kiss, and this was one of those times.

He backed up, looking startled. "I'm sorry. I shouldn't've done that."

"Probably not," Thea said, too stunned to move. "Not that I minded, but—"

"I know. Mixed signals."

"Uh, yeah."

She finally came to enough to grasp the door handle, but before she could escape Johnny said, "Not to pressure you or anything…but if you, you know, ever decide you…you'd rather not be alone—for the rest of the pregnancy, I mean—there's plenty of room up at the ranch."

"Thanks," she said, thinking, *Sure, torture me a little more, why not?* "But I'm fine. Really." She finally slid out of the truck, was halfway to her front door when he called out behind her, "If you want, I'll come with you to the flea market tomorrow."

Slowly, she turned, wondering if they'd slipped into some alternate universe while she'd been asleep. "Why on earth would you want to do that?"

"Because…because helping each other out is what friends do. Like you helped with Rach's wedding."

"Yeah," she said, chuckling, "except I enjoyed helping with the wedding. Somehow I can't picture you hawking painted wooden lizards to a bunch of *turistas*. You'll be bored out of your ever-loving mind within five minutes."

"Around you? Never happen. So what time should I pick you up?"

Dogs barked, birds sang, a freezy breeze blew, teasing her hair, her skin, her nipples. Or maybe that wasn't the breeze. "I'm usually outta here by seven-thirty at the latest," she said, giving up. Giving in.

"I'll be here at seven," he said, then drove off, leaving Thea wondering just what Ed had put in those hamburgers.

"And he actually did?" Winnie said, justifiably agog. For once, it was a true Girls' Day Out, all the postnatal progeny having been left with Tess's aunt over at Winnie's. Once the new crop of babies started popping out, however, it was anybody's guess when that would happen again.

"Honey," Thea said, setting a platter of loaded nachos in the center of the table, "the man was pimping my stuff like St. Peter himself was keeping tabs. What?" she said when Winnie and Tess exchanged a glance far more loaded than the nachos.

"Nothing, nothing," Tess said, trying to pick up a cheesy chip without messing up her new acrylics.

"Okay, look—" The chair scraped across the diner's worn vinyl floor when Thea pulled it out, then sank onto it. "I don't know what's going on any more than y'all. And I probably shouldn't've said anything, except since we were sitting in a public place for most of the day it wasn't exactly a secret." Annoyed, confused, she snatched a nacho off the platter, scooping up the biggest glob of cheese she could, along with a couple of jalapeños and a chunk of taco meat. Baby was gonna come out breathing fire. "It's just…"

"I know, sweetie," Tess said, all sympathy. "I know—"

"I had a cat like that once," Winnie said, thoughtfully licking gooey fingers. "Well, sorta. My grandmother wouldn't let me have an actual pet when I was a kid, but this stray kept hanging around, so I'd sneak him food whenever I could. He'd never let me get close, but he'd always show up at the corner of the yard, waiting. Once he even jumped in my open window and got on my bed. The second I tried to pet him, though—poof! So he wanted to be *around* me, as long as it was on his terms—"

"*Dios mio,* Winnie," Evangelista said as she and her bosoms waddled out from the kitchen. "You look like you're gonna explode! Now I know why you weren't in your regular booth, it'd take the Jaws of Life to get you out!"

"Geez, Ev—"

"It's okay, Thea," Winnie said, muttering naughty words when cheese dribbled all over a maternity top that could double as a parachute, "she's right. I got stuck in the bathtub last night. Aidan had to come haul me out. When he finally stopped laughing, that is."

Tess, who was all decked out in a hot little *waisted* sundress, the bitch, patted Winnie's hand.

"This, too, shall pass, honey. With Miguel, I got so fat at the end I couldn't roll over in bed by myself. Enrique had to help m-me…"

Winnie shifted her hand to grab hold of Tess's. "How long now?"

"January. We think. Hope." Tess lifted crossed fingers, not even bothering with a brave smile, although she sucked in a little breath before saying, "But back to you, *chica*—you think we should move up the shower date? Because *I'm* thinking you're not going to hold out for another month."

"From your lips to God's ears. But Robbie was two weeks

late, so no promises." This said with a grimace. "So please, somebody, anybody, tell me something to take my mind off the little parasite currently headbutting my bladder—"

"It's a girl!" Rachel shrieked from the doorway, God bless her exuberant soul, and Winnie said, "Okay, that'll do," and then they all descended on the newest member of their group with much hugging and kissing and congratulations, and Thea thought if it hadn't been for the whole Johnny-strangeness-thing, she'd be happy as a pig in slop. Her baby was fine, she was fine, she had good friends and her dogs and work that pleased her, so, all told, life was good. Very good, in fact.

So all she needed now, she thought as she walked back into her house a little later, was some way to squelch the constant, nagging little voice telling her it could be better, that *content* no longer meant the same thing it had before she got pregnant.

Because, suddenly, her crazy little home just seemed crazy and little, not adorably eccentric, the solitude she'd once cherished more of a cop-out than a choice. And none of her customary demon-banishing activities seemed to shake her out of her funk, not playing with the dogs or singing along with Elvis or even starting in on a new batch of painted critters.

Not that Johnny was a demon, but the images of him sure were, that sweet, unexpected kiss and him grinning like a goofball every time he scored a sale at the flea market and the way he'd kept up a one-sided conversation with the baby on the drive up to see her mother, and then Elvis started in singing "Can't Help Falling in Love with You," and she broke down sobbing, hurting for herself, hurting for Johnny, hurting for the elusive "them" they couldn't quite grasp.

Blubbering her eyes out, Thea twisted around and slid clumsily off her work stool to get a tissue, not seeing the fur-covered boulder at her feet. With a gasp, she went flying, careening off first that boulder, then another, barely catching herself on the back of the sofa before landing with a thud on her bottom.

"Oh, dear God," she whispered over the *whoosh-whoosh-whoosh* in her ears, hugging herself as dogs milled and wagged and whined, worried. "You okay, Itty-Bit?" The baby punched her a couple of times, like he was trying to get comfortable again after being so rudely jostled out of his nap.

She didn't move. Couldn't. All she could think was…what if the fall had been worse? What if she hadn't caught herself, or had broken something, or…

Or, or, or. The panicked thoughts rushed her like a swarm of spooked bats, bringing with them a new round of tears. Not because she was hurt, but because she was alone, the dogs notwithstanding. She looked at the lot of them, now mostly sitting and panting, waiting to see what she did next, and thought, *Adoring, yes, but not a Lassie in the bunch.*

Okay, so maybe this I'm-fine-on-my-own philosophy had its drawbacks.

The baby kicked, almost like he was trying to say *Ya think?*

He. Her little boy. Who expected his mama to take care of him until he was big enough to take care of himself. Someone who was probably wondering when she was gonna stop acting like a damn fool.

With a huge sigh, Thea hauled herself back to her feet, kicked her pride's big fat booty out of the way, and went to pack.

"Hey, boss," Carlos said, right after he and Johnny had bedded down the last of the mares and their foals for the night. The old man nodded toward the house. "Ain't that Miss Thea's Jeep?"

Johnny whipped around, squinting in the filmy, dusky light to see that, yep, that was Thea's Jeep, all right, complete with assorted dog heads hanging out the windows.

His heart banged against his rib cage.

By the time he reached the house, the front yard was writhing with canines, all of whom rushed him like he'd just returned from five years at sea. "Down," he commanded, and they backed off, looking at each other with *Who's the dude with the 'tude?* expressions that might have cracked him up if he hadn't been so focused on the pregnant woman in a T-shirt and overalls trying to haul a suitcase larger than she was out of the backseat.

"Man, the curbside service at this joint—" she wobbled dangerously when the car finally gave up the bag "—really sucks."

"Might've helped if you'd called ahead and made a reservation," Johnny said, gently setting her aside to get the rest of her things.

"Couldn't. Had to make my move before I changed my mind. You can get the cradle later, though...."

Crap, he thought when her voice cracked, letting go of the bag in his hands to grab her shoulders. "What happened? You okay?" His eyes dropped. "The baby—"

"Yeah, yeah, we're both okay. I just tripped over one of the dogs and—"

Johnny's grip tightened. "You *fell?*"

"Sorta. I kinda bounced off the sofa—and another dog—on my way down, so while it would've made a great YouTube video, I'm not hurt. Well, except for the boo-boo on my butt. But...but it scared the holy bejeebers out of me," she said in a small voice, and Johnny wrapped his arms around her, furious, terrified, relieved, making soft, "It's okay, nothing happened, you're safe now," noises as she began to tremble, a tiny, sweet-smelling earthquake against his chest.

"*S-safe* might be a matter of opinion," Thea said on a muffled chuckle, then pulled away, picking up one of the smaller cases. A light one, at least. "So congratulations. You won. I'm here." She cut through the herd of panting dogs toward the door. "At least until my belly no longer eclipses everything below it."

"Let's get one thing straight, right now," Johnny said, recoiling at the acrid stench of wounded pride trailing in her wake. He grabbed two of the cases and hauled ass up the stairs after her, kneeing aside dogs as he went. "I didn't *win* anything. You, and the baby, and your dogs—" five furry heads, all with pricked ears, swiveled to him at once "—can stay here as long as you like." On the porch landing, he frowned down at her. "You're also free to leave, anytime. But you'll be the one making the call. Not me. Got that?"

She almost smiled. "You might want to actually live under the same roof with me for more than five minutes before you paint yourself into that particular corner, okay? Come on, guys," she said to the dogs. "Let's check out the new digs."

Johnny'd barely caught the glimpse through the crack in Thea's self-esteem before her words sank in.

"Dogs live outside."

"Not in my world," she said sweetly, as five sets of paws trotted into his house, and the world—Johnny's world, anyway—tilted on its axis.

Chapter Ten

When he woke the next morning, he wasn't alone.

Unfortunately, although the creature snoring softly next to him smelled like Thea—somewhat—it was a lot hairier.

"Hey," Johnny said, poking the dog, who yawned and tried to give him a kiss.

"Forget it," he said, raising one arm to fend the thing off, which made the tongue go faster. He pointed to the door. *"Out!"*

The dog's *arf* of joy pierced his skull like a nail gun.

Thea appeared, hair sticking up, face sleep-creased, nipples extremely visible through the soft fabric of that hideously unsexy sack she was wearing, and Johnny's best friend let out an arf of joy, too.

"I'm so sorry, I had no idea he was in here," Thea said, padding across his rug in her bare feet to grab the dog's collar, making the sack mold to everything. *Maybe not so unsexy, after all,* he thought as the arfing turned into a moan. "Chuck!

Down!" she said, and the dog got down. Reluctantly. Johnny could relate. Especially when Thea's gaze latched onto his bare chest.

"You're staring," he said mildly, sitting up.

Her eyes lifted to his face. Eventually. "Damn."

Johnny brazenly eyed *her* chest. "I'll second that."

She glanced down, then back up. "It's cold."

"So I gathered." Yawning, he scratched his head, thinking that having Thea in his room at 6:00 a.m., all soft and round and sleep-flushed and unavailable, could make him grumpier than he already was, if he let it. "Have a good sleep?"

"As well as can be expected," she said, crossing her arms over those perky little nipples. She—and her furry friends—had basically passed out before nine. In the room across the hall. "Junior here would *not* let up, all night long. And my butt's got a bruise the size of Montana on it."

"You want me to kiss it and make it better?" Johnny said, his brain clearly having ceded the floor to the aforementioned best friend.

"Trust me, you kissing it would *not* make it better."

A pause.

"Is this going to be a problem for you?"

"Hell, yes," she said, then took her dog and her bruised butt and left.

At this rate, it'd be lunchtime before his jeans fit properly.

And wasn't this *little experiment starting out on an auspicious note?* Thea thought as she tromped back to her room, accepting that now that she—and her nipples—were up, going back to sleep was pointless. Grumpily, she fished out a sundress from one of her unpacked bags, did a quick wash in the adjoining bathroom and got dressed, thinking about how something could make perfect sense on paper and still not work worth beans in reality. Because sleeping across the hall from Johnny…imagining him in the altogether in that great big sleigh bed, all by his lonesome…

Bond, bond, bond, her hormones chanted.

She sighed, then called The Herd, leading them down the hall and through the kitchen to the back door. Ozzie was off today, but she'd poked around the kitchen last night to see what was what, decided sausage and pancakes would give her a reason for living.

As did the impossibly glorious morning, cool and cloudless, the rock outcroppings blushing in the sun's early-morning caress. Thea blushed a little herself as she and the dogs trooped down to the pond, well away from the house and the barns and Jess and Rach's cabin, remembering her reaction to Johnny earlier, and his to her.

So what harm would a little bone-jumping do?

"Hah," she said aloud, flushing a covey of quail out from a clump of thick, silvery-green sage, the roar of dozens of birds taking flight setting off five dogs' insane—and completely ineffectual—barking. The baby kicked, like he wanted to get in on the action: Thea had a sudden image of a little boy laughing and clapping his hands at the sight of the birds' liftoff, and her eyes teared.

She cautiously lowered herself cross-legged onto the ground, watching the sun sparkle on the shimmering water as the dogs variously explored or chased each other or simply flopped down beside her, keeping her company, and felt more at peace than she could ever remember being, even though there was nothing even remotely peaceful about her situation—

"Hey," she heard behind her, and she thought, *Speaking of which.* She twisted around—as best she could—to see Johnny approaching her, his hat shadowing his face, and again it occurred to her how much alike they were, at least in this. How much they'd both let the past shape them, determine who they were and the choices they made. How afraid they both were of something most people took for granted—the basic human need to love. And be loved. And as he squatted beside her, smiling slightly, something flared to life inside her brain, that how on earth did she expect to receive love when she was being so stingy with it herself?

She could almost see her mother's Now *do you get it?* raised eyebrow.

Well, hell.

"How'd you find me?" she asked as Johnny sat beside her.

"Saw you head this way while I was getting dressed."

"Don't you have horses to tend to?"

"Carlos can handle it." He hesitated, then said, "If I'm invading your space or whatever..."

"No, no...it's fine," she said, even as *Please. Invade my space* played on through.

Johnny nodded. "I just wanted to make sure you were okay. I don't mean physically," he added at her frown. "About you moving in with me. Because this must be awkward as hell for you."

For a moment, she watched his profile, wondering why the big goof felt it necessary to apologize for his generosity. "No more than it is for you, I imagine."

"Oh, I'm fine," he said, and she thought, *Suuure you are,* even as a sudden, terrifying, paradigm-shifting thought rose up in Thea's brain.

Facing the water again, she sucked in a deep breath, held on to it for a moment, then let it out on, "You're right. This is never going to work."

"Thea—"

"Because sharing a house, a child..." She picked up a stick and hurled it toward the pond. Four out of five dogs went after it. "And a bed, because I don't think either of us is delusional enough to think that's not gonna happen..." She looked at him, swallowing down the terror. "Seems to me we may as well make it legal."

Silence. "As in...getting married?"

"Yep. Unless you've changed your mind?"

"No. No! It's just..." Johnny gave his head a sharp shake, then got to his feet. Walked away. Turned back, frowning. "You sure? I mean, after everything you said..."

Thea shielded her eyes to get a better look at his, making sure she wasn't imagining...well, maybe not panic, exactly, but a cousin once or twice removed.

And wouldn't that be a kick in the pants, if, after all this time, he'd decided she'd been right all along? That getting hitched *wasn't* a good idea? Even so, she knew calling him on it would be pointless. For one thing, he'd deny it up one side and down the other; for another, his integrity would never allow him to renege on an offer, once he'd made it.

"Assuming I get the standard seventy-two hours to cancel without penalty?" she said mildly. "Yeah. I'm sure."

The panic eased off a little, she thought, as Johnny sat again, this time leaning against a cottonwood trunk a few feet away. The warm, hay-scented breeze ruffled his hair, his shirt, tortured her with his scent, as a heavily panting Franny and J.D. came trotting back and flopped down beside her. Johnny frowned at the dogs for a moment, then asked, simply, "Why?"

Thea stared hard at Franny's speckled tummy as she scratched it. "I could say I decided it's like you said, that this isn't about what I want—what either of us wants—it's about what's best for our son. And letting pride, or fear, or whatever it was keeping me saying 'no' all these months get in the way of that..." She swiped a stray hair out of her eyes. "That's not the kind of mama I want to be. But while that wouldn't be a lie, it wouldn't be the whole truth, either."

"No?"

"No. Because I realized I'm fighting a losing battle." Meeting his eyes dead on, she said, her voice amazingly steady, "I'm guessing you're not gonna be real thrilled about this, but...hard as I tried not to fall in love with you, it didn't work."

Johnny got real quiet. No surprise there. "Oh," he said, and her heart cramped a little, that nothing had changed on that score, but then she remembered she was playing by new rules now, and her heart rallied.

"Yeah. *Oh.* So that's the deal. If we get married, it's with the full understanding that I love you. And I'm not gonna pretend otherwise." She angled her head, trying to see his face. "How's that going down, then?"

Laughing softly, Johnny said, "Too soon to tell." Then he removed his hat to scratch his head, the silver threads in his hair shining like tiny beacons in the bright sun. "Don't know which one of us this is scarier for."

"Tell me about it. But at least we can't say we're going into this blind."

After a moment, his lips curved. "No, we sure can't."

"You...want to think this over?"

This time, Thea could actually see him wrestling with the panic, see it flare, then recede, in his eyes. "What's to think about?" he said at last. "Other than setting a date? When's good for you?"

"I'm seven months pregnant," she said, doing a little wrestling herself. "I'm thinking soon."

"Soon works for me. Come here," he said, crunching forward to help her skootch backward against his chest, his corded arms encircling her from behind, and he smelled so fresh-from-the-shower good her eyes crossed. Then a chuckle tickled her back. "You sure you don't want to get married just so we can fool around?"

"Oh, right. Do I look like a born-again virgin?"

"What you look like," he said, his breath sending goose bumps hoppity-skipping along her skin, "is the sexiest woman on God's green earth."

"That's just the sun in your eyes."

"No sun—I'm in the shade. Which is why it's killed me, not to be able to touch you all these months. But you didn't want it, so I didn't push."

"Who said I didn't want it?" Thea said, relaxing into Johnny's embrace. Goodness gracious, all this sex talk was making her warm. And willing. "Just didn't seem like a good idea at the time." She grimaced at her stomach. "Now I'm not sure how—"

"Not to worry," Johnny said, shifting her to bring their mouths together in a kiss expressly designed to rid one of pesky things like performance anxiety because you felt like an elephant. Except as nice as it was, and as turned on as she was getting, she could practically taste the tension and apprehension on his lips.

"What?" he said when she planted a hand on his chest. His face fell. "Please, *please* don't tell me you changed your mind again."

"It's not me who's got issues with this, it's you. Not about having sex—it's obvious you're raring to go on that score. It's all the rest of it. And don't tell me I'm imagining things, because I know you too well."

When he turned slightly, Thea lifted her knuckles to his cheek, rough even though he'd just shaved. She waited until his eyes met hers, though, before she said, "Johnny, I do know what I'm getting into—"

"No, you don't—"

"Yes, I do. And I know who I'm marrying, which I sure as

heck didn't the last time I did this. There's a lot to be said for being respected. For being treated right. For being with somebody I can *trust.* And maybe that's far more important than what I thought I wanted." She stretched to brush her lips over his, letting her tongue graze his bottom lip, a move she knew drove him crazy. "I want this, honey," she whispered. "I want you." And this time, when he drove his hands through her hair and joined his open mouth to hers, it was like before, only better, somehow. Richer. Like they'd moved from black and white into color.

From pretend into real. As real as they were gonna get, anyway.

Then she was on her back, cushioned by who knew how many years of leaf mold, even as Johnny carefully cupped her head to keep stuff out of her hair as the spit-swapping got more serious and her nipples zing-a-linged and her Very Special Place reminded her exactly how long it'd been since anybody'd treated *it* right. Whimpering and moaning and generally acting like a pregnant woman who hadn't had sex in seven months, Thea wound her arms around Johnny's neck and let him have at it, even as it occurred to her they were having at it where God and any old body could see them.

Then Johnny started messing with her nipple right through her dress and her dumb cotton maternity bra and she yelped, and he chuckled, and she said, "Um, not to break the mood or anything? But I was kinda thinking in terms of, you know, in private?" and he said, "Sign says right at the end of the road, Private Property," and she would've hit him except he had her hands up over her head and her dress rucked up and…

"Huh," he said, frowning, "I'm taking it Victoria's Secret doesn't cater to pregnant gals?"

"Not last time I checked, no. Although I'm guessing they've helped more'n one woman *get* pregnant." She gasped as the cool breeze lapped at her now-exposed nipples. "Hated the bra, did you?"

"It's fine. Just in my way."

"You can stop grinning now."

"No way. Holy hell…where'd those come from?"

"You, actually. But don't get excited, I still don't fill out a B," she murmured, adding, as he lifted her hips and first the breeze, then Johnny, licked at her nether regions, "Take it those were in your way, too?"

"You might say," he whispered across a spot where the sun didn't *generally* shine, which might've been a lot more thrilling if—

"Can't…breathe," she choked out, and Johnny said, "Right, forgot about that," and somehow flipped her ungainly self so that she was straddling him, her dress floating back down over her breasts as well as Johnny's hands, which were doing things to her nipples that made her giddy with pleasure, aided not inconsiderably by what was pressing into her swollen, and very grateful, hoo-ha, and while Thea generally held leisurely foreplay in the highest regard, this was not one of those times.

"Good now?" Johnny asked.

"Could be better," she muttered, writhing, her hands planted on his chest as she tried to focus on his slowly blossoming grin, and she remembered—much too late—why she'd resisted this so hard, because she'd moved past the sex-is-just-sex thing with him a long time ago. He angled himself to tongue a breast through the fabric and she ground out, "Keep doing that and they're gonna h-hear me in three counties."

"You that close already?"

"Honey, I've been close for months," she said, and he lifted her up just enough to unzip, and then glory halle*lu*jah he was inside her, and she thought, *Regrets not allowed,* and a second later she wasn't thinking at all, she was just enjoying the heck out of the ride, even as it vaguely registered that the dogs were all looking away, embarrassed.

Laughing, dizzy, amazed, she shuddered into one giant, shimmering orgasm, her own devouring Johnny's as he followed her lead, their cries sending another quail covey exploding from the brush. Her heart pounding, her palms still on Johnny's chest, Thea slowly opened her eyes…and burst out laughing.

Slowly, his eyes closed, Johnny grinned. Underneath her palms, his heart was doing a pretty good samba of its own. "Think of it as our way of announcing our engagement," he said, as first Norma Jean, then Bugly, cautiously sniffed them, making sure they hadn't killed each other. And she would have laughed again if his grin hadn't faded far more quickly than it'd bloomed. Frowning slightly herself, Thea skimmed her fingertips over his cheekbone. *Stay with me,* she thought, even though technically he still was. "What?" she whispered.

But all he did was gently lift her off to set about rearranging himself, tossing Thea her panties in the process.

"Talk about your short afterglows," she said, hearing the unnatural brightness in her voice as she rehooked her bra.

"Somebody's coming at ten to look over a couple of the fillies. I need to shower again, get breakfast—"

"I thought I'd do sausage and pancakes, if that's okay."

He gave her a hard look. "You're not here as a housekeeper, Thea."

"Well aware of that, bucko. But since Ozzie's off today, and a bowl of cereal ain't gonna cut it, I figured I'd make breakfast. No big deal."

More of the hard-look thing preceded his helping her to her feet. But although he took her hand as they walked back to the house, trailed by a stream of dogs, Thea could feel the tension in his grasp, see it in the way he avoided meeting her eyes. She yanked him back around, hurling, "What's wrong?" at his frown.

The flinch was slight, but she still caught it. "Wrong?" He laughed. Sort of. "What on earth could be wrong? I just had totally unexpected, mind-blowing sex with the hottest woman in the state. Believe me," he rumbled, lifting her hand to his mouth to drag his bottom lip across her knuckles, "I haven't been this right in a very, very long time." And she almost lost it all over again, until it dawned on her how easily the man could use sex to distract her from, well, pretty much everything, and that she'd been there a time or six before and damned if she was going there again. With anybody.

So she steeled herself against the hundred million clearly insatiable hormones threatening to melt her brain and said, "But you'd tell me if something was bugging you, right?" and yep, there went the flinch again. Maybe only in his eyelids, but still.

"Nothing's bugging me, Thea. And yes, pancakes and sausage would be great, thanks."

Liar, she thought as they trooped back to the house. Maybe she'd let him inside her, but he didn't seem any too anxious to return the favor.

Clearly, this was gonna be harder than she'd thought.

They were married a week later, in a no-frills City Hall ceremony in Santa Fe with just Rachel and Jess, and Thea's mother and her husband in attendance. Johnny had been more than willing to go with something fancier, but Thea'd said she'd done the white-dress-and-bridesmaids route once before, and look how that'd turned out. She hadn't worn jeans, though, instead opting for a pretty, light orange dress that made her look like a supersize scoop of peach ice cream. And Ed and Sheila had insisted on springing for lunch at one of the City Different's swankier hotels, where they were spending the night as well.

Truth be told, Johnny felt like a complete yokel in the posh surroundings. Thea, however—the cushy, one-size-fits-all robe straining to cover her belly—took to room service and minibars like she was born to them.

"Now this is what I call a honeymoon," she said, sitting crossed-legged in the middle of the king-size bed and popping a chilled shrimp into her grinning mouth.

"One night in a hotel less than fifty miles from home?"

"Sure as hell beats a camping trip."

"Ouch."

"And what's even sorrier is that I thought it was romantic," she said, provoking a spike of annoyance, that her ex hadn't even treated her right on their honeymoon, for God's sake. And right on its heels, another spike, this time of guilt. Thea's brow creased as another shrimp met its fate. "You're not eating?"

"Some of us are still only eating for one," he said, and she swatted a hand at him. And dispatched another shrimp. "Did you hear Mama say Ed told her they could move down here if she wanted, so she could be closer to her grandbaby?"

"I did." Johnny smiled slightly. "You okay with that?"

"Yeah. I am." Frowning slightly, she reached for a glass of iced tea on the nightstand. "I just wish—"

"What?"

"That I'd understood her sooner, that's all." She blinked a few times, then took a sip of her tea before setting it back on the nightstand. "Wasn't until I had her again that I realized how much I've m-missed her. How stupid I've been."

Johnny sat beside her, folding her into his arms while she went on. "Mama did her best, you know? Did what she thought was best. Only I was too wrapped up in my own issues to understand that. If I turn out to be half the mother she was—is—I'll be doing okay."

After a moment, Johnny said, "From where I'm sitting, you've got absolutely nothing to worry about."

She tilted her head to give him a little smile. "Thanks." Then she frowned. "You never talk about your mother. Must've been hard, losing her so young. You ever miss her?"

"She's been gone a long time," Johnny said quietly, smiling at Thea's slight scowl when he removed the bowl of shrimp. Then, slowly, Thea's robe, thoroughly kissing first one pale shoulder, then the other. "And this is not appropriate honeymoon conversation."

"True," she said, sliding all the way out of the robe to stretch out in a pool of late-day sunshine, like she was bathing in liquid gold. Kat had always been self-conscious about her pregnant body, hated him seeing her naked. Thea reveled in it, maybe because of everything she'd gone through to get here, he didn't know.

Without fanfare, Johnny stood and stripped, so hungry for her he ached, even as he knew the ache was for more than Thea's body, it was for her substance, for whatever it was that made her her—her resilience and strength and deep, deep reserves of love that apparently nothing could quench.

He wanted to drink from her. Absorb her. He wanted, period, he thought as he crawled into bed behind her, curling around her warmth to palm a surprisingly cool, soft breast, the small pink nipple already as hard as he was. "Man," she murmured, arching her back to cup the back of his head. "You sure know how to make a pregnant lady feel sexy."

"I do my best," he murmured, dodging the jeering memory. "What do you say we prove all those idiots wrong who insist married sex is boring?"

"Count me in," she said, flopping over to face him, pressing kisses to his neck and chest, making him feel greedy. Selfish.

"Slow or fast?" he asked.

Thea hoisted herself up onto one elbow to gently rake her fingers through his hair, her smile soft, her eyes so full of love Johnny's stung. She leaned in, kissed him, tasting of fresh shrimp and tangy cocktail sauce. "How's about we just go for it and see where we end up, 'kay?" she said, and he thought, *Can't do this, can't...*

"Roll back over."

One side of her mouth lifted. "Am I gonna like this?"

"Trust me," he said, the words bitter in his mouth.

"So that's how that works," Thea said. Much later.

"Yep," Johnny said, still behind her. Still with the hand on the breast.

She grazed his knuckles with one fingertip. "You're gonna be disappointed when they go flat again after the baby comes."

"Somehow I doubt it."

"Oh, trust me...they'll deflate, all right."

He chuckled softly. "No, that I'll be disappointed."

But there was an edge to his chuckle that made her twist around. "Johnny—"

"Shh," he said, kissing her again before spooning her more tightly, his breath soft on her temple. "Afterglow, remember?"

Let it lie, she thought. *Let it—*

"So this probably isn't a good time to ask if you're having second thoughts?"

Predictably, he tensed. "No, it isn't. And why on earth would you think that, anyway?"

"Because there's a reason you wouldn't look at me?"

"You being that pregnant kinda limited my options."

"That's not the reason, Johnny. And we both know it."

His hot sigh singed her shoulder. "I'm not having second thoughts, honey."

"Oh, no?" She struggled out of his arms to face him,

'hether he liked it or not. "I know we tap-danced around the 'ove' part of our vows today, but we did promise to respect nd be there for each other. And to be honest. So, yeah, I uppose since this is our honeymoon and all, I could pretend verything's fine." She cupped his jaw, locking their eyes. Except you're not doing such a hot job of it, either."

After a moment, he sat up, the sheet draped across his lap. You really think I can make you happy?" Dark, definitely oncerned eyes met hers. "In the long run, I mean?"

"Honestly, Johnny," Thea said over the lump in her throat, ickling her fingers down his bare arm. "I told you, I went nto this with my eyes wide open. And right now," she said, ushing herself up enough to kiss his firm, gorgeous bicep, he plus column far outweighs the minus."

"And what happens when that balance shifts?" he asked uietly, and there it was again, the ugly, trembling creature owering in the corner.

"Not gonna happen," she said, more to the creature than to im. "Because I won't let it."

At his sad smile, Thea sat up enough to wrap her arms round her husband, thinking, *Go away, leave him alone, he's ine*...silently promising Johnny she'd hold on tight until the eature either left, or she killed it.

Either way was fine by her.

Chapter Eleven

The sun wasn't even full up yet when Johnny walked throug
the back door to the smells of coffee brewing and bacc
frying, to the sight of his very pregnant wife, already in h
waitress getup, standing at the stove and singing along wi
some country-western *hombre* on Ozzie's old radio.

Despite a dog or three padding over to greet him, Thea didn
hear him right away, affording him the opportunity to savor t
way the strands of pale blond hair that had escaped her ponyta
tickled her neck and shoulders, to once more marvel that, fro
the back, you couldn't tell she was even pregnant, even thoug
she still ate like a plague of locusts. To smile at how what s
lacked in any real musical talent she made up for in enthusias
As usual, a mix of tenderness and aggravation shudder
through him, as, not for the first time since their marriage tw
weeks before, he found himself wondering how a pers
could find himself living in heaven and hell at the same tim

How victory could be both so sweet and so frightening.

It scared him, how quickly he'd gotten used to having her around. How much he missed her when she wasn't. He'd even gotten used to the dogs. Somewhat. What he couldn't get used to was the almost constant tightness in his chest, not of wanting what he couldn't have, but of having what he didn't dare let himself want.

Franny, the one with the big ears, woofed at him, making Thea spin around, her belly almost knocking her off balance. "Hey," she said, her smile soft as she tucked one of those strands behind her ear. "You're up early this morning."

"Went riding," he said, crossing to the coffeemaker, pouring himself a cup. "Why're you awake? Thought you didn't go in until seven these days?"

She shrugged, her arm stretched to turn the sizzling, popping bacon. "Got too warm under the quilt. It woke me up."

"Sorry. Way you were all curled up, you looked cold." Cold, and beautiful, and vulnerable in sleep in a way she sure as hell never looked awake.

"I probably was," she said, tossing him a grin. "But I get hot real fast these days."

"So I've noticed," he said, and she rolled her eyes, snorting a laugh through her nose. Johnny took a slug of his coffee, then said, carefully, "Thought you were gonna quit soon."

"I am." She transferred first one, then another, piece of bacon onto a paper towel to crisp. "It's just not 'soon' yet. And don't give me that look, we've had this conversation before."

"And we're gonna keep havin' it until you see sense."

"What? You gonna *make* me quit working?"

Johnny had to smile. "I'm not that stupid."

"Didn't think you were. And anyway, waiting tables is nothing compared to what you put me through last night. And this morning."

"What I put *you* through?" She laughed; he blew out a breath. "You do realize our sex life's gonna take a huge hit once this little guy's made his appearance?"

"All the more reason to stockpile the memories for the lean years." She cracked four eggs into a bowl, took a whisk to them while dogs looked on, forlorn. And Johnny took another swallow of his coffee, watching his wife, his feelings so mixed up he could hardly tell them apart.

Oh, yeah—the sex was as good as ever. Better. But only a fool would deny the uneasiness buzzing underneath the surface. Maybe Thea'd backed off with the "getting in touch with his feelings" thing, but for how long?

"Sit. Eat," she said a moment later when the eggs were done. "Toast will be ready in a sec."

"You don't have to wait on me," Johnny grumbled, dropping into a kitchen chair and setting his mug on the table.

"And if I didn't," she said, setting two plates on the table, "you'd starve. Okay, maybe not starve," she added at his frown, "but close. And anyway, I like having somebody to cook for. So deal."

"God, Thea—I don't deserve you."

Like disturbed ghosts, the words flew from his mouth, hovering between them, confused and startled. Heat licking at his face, Johnny lowered his eyes and shoveled in a bite of eggs. The toaster popped; ignoring it, Thea instead gently cupped the back of his head.

"Think maybe you got that backward, honeybunch," she said, dropping a kiss on his forehead before turtling toward the toaster, and the ghosts shuffled off, leaving Johnny to wonder how on earth she managed to get food to her customers before it got cold.

Frankly, Johnny was surprised Evangelista hadn't given her the boot already. Of course, when he'd tried putting a word in the woman's ear, she'd nearly bitten off his head, telling him Thea could damn well make up her own mind when she was ready to go on maternity leave and he could damn well mind his own business. Nor was Naomi any help, insisting that as long as Thea felt okay and her blood pressure stayed down, working was actually good for her.

Women, he thought morosely, chewing his bacon, his thoughts interrupted when Thea set down a plate with four pieces of toast and suddenly said, "Would you teach me to ride? After the baby comes, I mean." She grinned. "Obviously."

His forehead crimped, he watched her sloooowly lower herself to her chair. "Hate to break it to you, but you have to actually get close to a horse before you can ride it."

"Yeah, I thought of that. So I decided to think of them as big dogs. That I can sit on. Because what kind of sorry-ass horseman's wife is afraid of horses?"

"You're also afraid of heights."

"You *would* bring that up," she said, pulling a face as she chewed. Then she sighed. "Fears are bitches, aren't they?"

"Fear keeps you safe," Johnny mumbled into his coffee.

"Common sense keeps you safe," Thea said, a little too meaningfully for his taste. "Fear keeps you from living."

"Depends on how you define *living.*"

"This is true," she said, checking her watch. "Damn—how did it get so late?" Her last two bites of egg inhaled, she pushed herself to her feet, kissed him like she'd never see him again, then trundled over to the counter by the back door to get her purse and car keys. "And in the name of gender equality, you can clean up, how's that? Oh—and don't forget, I've got Winnie's baby shower at Tess's after work, so I won't be home until suppertime."

"Speaking of Tess," Johnny said, standing to clear the table, "the two of you do anything yet about putting your old place up for sale?"

"We're working on it," she said, avoiding his eyes, then gave him a little wave as she opened the back door, his bubbly daughter popped in and Johnny nearly had a heart attack.

"Hey, honey," Thea said, giving her stepdaughter a hug. "Your father's going to teach me to ride, isn't that great?"

"Now?"

"No, of course not now, later—"

"What the *hell* are you wearing?"

"Annnd that's my cue to leave," Thea said, pulling the door shut behind her.

"Chill, Dad," Rachel said, zeroing in on the leftover bacon on the stove. Shoving a piece into her mouth, her other hand palmed her now unmistakable bump, bared for all the world to see between a too-small tank top and a pair of stretchy black pants that clearly didn't stretch far enough. "I was out speed walking, decided to stop by on the off chance somebody'd made breakfast." She lifted another piece of bacon in a salute. "Score!" Then she frowned at Johnny. "What's with you?"

"Nothing," he growled, now close enough to the stove to see it was a holy mess. The dogs were doing a fair job of pre-cleaning whatever they could reach, but everything else was his. Then his daughter's words sank in. "You were what?"

"Speed walking. So I don't turn into a tub o' lard by the end of this thing." Grinning, she ganked the last slice of bacon off the grease-spotted paper towel, making Johnny—who'd been eyeing that piece of bacon for the last ten minutes—even grumpier.

Sunk into a comfy armchair in Tess's tiny living room, Thea did the happy-face thing as Winnie opened her shower gifts, trying not to dwell on Johnny's little "I don't deserve you" number that morning. Had the words been delivered with a wink and a grin, she would've thought no more about it. But they hadn't. And his deep blush afterward… Oh, dear God—

"When are you due again?" Rachel asked Winnie from the floor at Thea's feet, where she kept an eagle eye on nine-month-old Julia to make sure she didn't eat any of the discarded wrappings.

"Basically any minute," Winnie said, accepting a paper plate loaded with munchies from Tess's aunt Flo. "Naomi said I'm already three centimeters dilated and 50 percent effaced."

"Hell, honey," Tess said, "one good sneeze and you're done."

"Don't I wish. My first labor was eighteen hours…"

And thence ensued the one constant at every baby shower since the first cavewomen gathered to bestow the newest Neanderthal with pelts to sleep under and bones to gnaw: birthing stories, each woman determined to top the one before her, either with how fast and "easy" her labor had been, or how long and torturous. At one point, Rachel reached up to slip her hand into Thea's, meeting her gaze with great big I'd-kinda-forgotten-about-that-part eyes.

Except then she leaned closer, whispering, "I think you and I need to pay a visit to the little girl's room," and Thea said, "No, I'm fine," and Rachel said, "No, you're not," and got up—still nimbly, damn her—to haul Thea out of the chair and down the hall to Tess's quiet, deeply carpeted bedroom and its massive master bath with the double sinks, huge sunken bathtub and separate water closet. A good thing, since Thea was not into communal peeing.

"Wow," Rachel said. "Totally not what I expected."

Since this would be Enrique's last tour of duty—they fervently hoped—he and Tess had decided that she and Miguel should move back to Tierra Rosa for the duration rather than Tess living on or near Enrique's home base in Texas. However, what had started life as a modest '70s ranch was slowly morphing into something worthy of one those blended-name celebrity couples.

"Tess had the bathroom remodeled after she sold that wonker house down in Santa Fe to some Hollywood honcho. A producer or somebody. As a surprise for Enrique when he comes home, she said."

"Huh," Rachel said, ducking into the potty first, only pushing the door partway closed so she could call out through the crack, "Anyway…I don't know which of you looks crankier today—you or Dad."

"I'm gonna say your father," Thea said, redoing her saggy ponytail. "'Cause I'm not grumpy. I'm pregnant."

The toilet flushed; Rachel emerged to wash her hands at one of the distressed copper sinks. "I'm pregnant, too, but I don't go around scowling all the time." *That's because… Oh, what's the use, she can't help being young,* Thea thought as Rachel looked at her in the mirror. "Silly me," she said, flicking water off her hands, "I thought maybe marriage would smooth things out between you and Dad."

"Why on earth would you think that?"

"Like I said."

In response to her bladder's Pavlovian response to being near a toilet, Thea plodded toward the water closet. "What can I say? Marriage isn't always a basket of daffodils." Having contributed her two drops, she flushed, nearly doing herself in trying to get her maternity shorts back up. "At least," she said as she came out, "it isn't for most of us poor slobs."

"I do know that, Thea," Rachel said over the running water as Thea washed her hands. "It's not like Jess and I don't fight from time to time. And don't you dare tell Dad I said that."

Drying her hands on a minuscule hand towel, Thea frowned at the younger woman. "You fight?"

"Omigod, just yesterday we had this blowup you would not *believe* about politics. Because he said—"

"You fight about *politics?*"

"Duh, we always have. We were, like, the only two kids in school who even cared, which is so sad. Anyway, we ended up spending, like, hours on the computer, looking up stuff to back up our arguments. And eventually we agreed we each had a valid point. But my point is…it's okay to fight as long as you listen to each other. As long as you remember that your relationship is always more important than whatever you're fighting about."

"Uh-huh. And doesn't that sound like a commercial for why your father and I should go see your marriage guru."

"It wouldn't hurt."

"Like there's a chance in hell Johnny Griego would agree to such a thing."

Rachel's head snapped around, tears cresting on her lower lashes. "And ever since our trip to the mall, I've been thinking about what you said, about me wanting things to work out between you and Dad so *I'd* feel better. At first it really pissed me off you'd even think that. But the more I thought about it, the more I realized it was true. At least, it was then."

Palming the neat little mound underneath her baggy T-shirt, she added, "But honest to God, this isn't only about me. Next to Jess, and this baby, Dad and you are more important to me than anybody. Yeah, Mom fits in there, too, except…well, you know what I mean. Anyway, first you were so against this marriage, and then suddenly you changed your mind, and now I get the feeling you're regretting it or something, and Dad's all agitated, too, and swear to God, if he ends up hurt again on account of you—"

"What?" Thea whirled on her, her eyebrows up by her

hairline. "Honey, I admire your loyalty, and I understand why you're concerned—I think—but haven't you got the wrong end of the stick? Because who do you think's taking the bigger risk here? Me or your father?"

"So this isn't some marriage of convenience?"

"To be honest, at the moment I'm not sure what it is. And I doubt your dad has a clue, either. But you know what? Maybe you should give me—give *us*—a chance to work this out at our own speed, the way we've gotta work this out. And you badgering us isn't gonna make that happen any faster. Or with any better results."

A slight frown marred Rachel's forehead. "You're really committed to this, then?"

Sighing, Thea slung one arm around the girl's waist and steered her back into Tess's bedroom. "God knows I have no idea how this is going to turn out. Or *if,* to be perfectly honest. But whatever the outcome, it's not gonna happen overnight."

Before they reached the door to the hall, Thea faced her stepdaughter again and grasped her hands. "I love your father, honey. So I'm asking you to trust me—"

A shriek from the living room sent Rachel flying and Thea waddling down the hall. By the time she got there, a dozen women were darting about and jabbering and making phone calls and generally acting like a naked man had just streaked through the room.

"This is supposed to be a shower, *chica,*" Tess said as she and her aunt hefted a panting Winnie to her feet. "Not a flood."

"Winnie's water just broke," Rachel said, next door to stunned. "All over Tess's couch."

Except, as she guided Winnie toward her door, Tess said, "Oh, what the hell, it just gives me an excuse to get a new one, right?" and Thea started laughing so hard she half thought she'd pop out her own baby.

"You!" Tess barked. "On the tile! 'Cause I am not replacing the carpet, you hear me?"

"Omigosh…" Thea tucked two-day-old Seamus Black into the crook of her arm and sank farther into Winnie's leather sofa, willing her own little bundle of joy not to send a sharp right hook to the baby's tiny butt. She swallowed, steadying her voice. "He's absolutely gorgeous."

Perched beside her on the chair arm, Johnny carefully cupped the baby's head with a slightly trembling hand, the tender gesture bringing a lump to Thea's throat. His horses, a baby, his daughter…them, he could love, no problem. His wife, however…

Thea shut her eyes. *Patience, chickie, patience.*

"I'd forgotten how small they start out," Johnny said.

Across from them, Winnie barked out a laugh. "Small, my butt. Nine pounds, six ounces, ninety percent of it head. Yee-ouch."

"And we'll hear no complaints from you," Aidan said as he came into the room. "You were the one insisting on a natural birth, that y'didn't want to miss a single second of the experience." The shaggy-haired giant released an exaggerated sigh. "The way she near to broke my hand, I was about to ask if they'd give *me* the drugs instead," he said, ducking when Winnie took a harmless swipe at him.

"Not me, boy," Thea said, her eyes dipping back to the baby when Aidan planted a quick kiss on his wife's mouth. "I want every drug they got, long as it doesn't harm the baby. Knock me out and wake me up when the kid's here would be fine with me."

"Wuss," Winnie said, smiling.

"You bet."

Little Seamus started to fuss; an obviously besotted Aidan immediately scooped his new son out of Thea's arms to hand him over to Winnie, who discreetly tucked the "wee lad" underneath her blouse to nurse him. *Beatific* was the only word to describe the new mother's smile when she returned her gaze to Thea's, silently sharing the bond of those who'd almost given up on dreams coming true.

Shaken, Thea stood, leaning over to give Winnie a hug and the baby a last, lingering look. "We'll leave you to your bonding, then."

"But you haven't been here ten minutes!"

"It's not like either of us is going anywhere. And there's my baby shower next week, anyway."

"You wait that long to come see us and there'll be hell to pay," Winnie said, so Thea promised she'd be by in a day or two, gave Aidan a hug, waited while the two men shook hands, then got out of there as quickly as she dared without looking rude.

Because, truth be told, she felt like a bratty kid with a roomful of toys who only wanted the one the other kid had. Except that wasn't quite it, either, because this wasn't just about feeling left out or deprived. It was about desperately wanting to know how to erase the ever-present troubled look in Johnny's eyes…wanting to know why, as good as the sex was, Johnny was clearly uncomfortable whenever she tried to be simply affectionate with him.

Why, in a weird sort of way, he seemed to be almost afraid of her.

"That's gotta be some kind of record," Johnny said, cutting the engine when they got back to the ranch. "Twenty minutes without you saying a single word." He shook his head, grinning. "Scary."

No, what was scary was how things could be so easy between them one minute, so tense the next. "Just thinkin' about the baby," she fibbed. "This one, I mean, not Winnie's."

Johnny hesitated, then touched the back of his hand to her cheek. Let her try the same thing, though—

"Finally gettin' excited?"

"Guess so." She paused. "Does…the worry ever completely go away?"

"You have the nerve to ask me that after what Rach just put me through? Is *still* putting me through?" When Thea pulled a face, he chuckled. "Welcome to parenthood. Although, to be fair, there is the occasional ten-minute stretch when you're just too tired to give a damn."

"Something to look forward to, then," Thea said, unlatching her seat belt. By the time she got everything facing the same direction, though, Johnny had opened her door to help her out. At this point, it was either let him or fall out of the truck. Except once back on terra firma, she muttered, "Is it me, or is the front door farther away than it was this morning— Oh!"

"What is it?"

"No worries, just a Braxton Hicks," she hissed through her teeth as her muscles spazzed, blowing out a breath after it passed. "All better… What are you doing?" she said when Johnny swept her into his arms.

"Carrying you to the house."

"Be…cause?"

"Because I'd like to get there sometime this year."

"I'd make it eventually, you know."

"Well, now you'll make it faster."

Thea looped her hands around her husband's neck, studying the side of his face. Inhaling him. Marveling at the ease with which he carried her across the yard and onto the porch.

Resisting the urge to do the girly-girl thing and lay her head on his chest. "By the way…I gave notice to Evangelista today."

That merited the Frown of Disbelief. "Really?"

"Yeah. When it took so long to get Abe Pritchard's enchiladas to him, they were cold, I figured it was time…. What's so funny?"

"Nothing," he said, his mouth twitching.

"Actually, you have no idea how much it pains me to say this, but…" He set her down to open the door. Dogs rushed past them to pee, bark at the wind, whatever. "I should've quit weeks ago."

"*Real*ly?"

"You're totally enjoying this, aren't you?"

"You have no idea."

Sighing, Thea followed him inside. "Okay, so maybe I was being a tiny bit stubborn. Why didn't somebody tell me how miserable I was gonna be?"

No reply. "Hey," she said to his back, "we haven't been married nearly long enough for you to be tuning me out already."

"I assumed the question was rhetorical," Johnny said, unabashed. "Especially since I'm guessing more'n one woman did tell you exactly that—"

"There you are," Ozzie said, magically appearing like a genie, a dish towel tucked into his waistband. As much as Thea loved to cook, she had to admit Ozzie's days "on" were her fave days of the week. "Supper's nearly ready. Chicken 'n' dumplings. You got ten minutes. And how was that beautiful new baby?"

"Sleepy," Johnny said, then asked, "Rach and Jess eating here tonight?"

"No, she called a little while ago, said she and Jess 'had plans.' So it's just us tonight. Carlos already ate." Ozzie frowned at Thea. "You feeling okay?"

"She just had one of those…things," Johnny said with an unconvinced frown. "A fake contraction?"

"Guys, I'm fine—"

"Oh, yeah, Dee used to get those all the time. Got so bad with the last one I didn't believe her when she went into real labor. She nearly dropped the kid in the front yard as we was goin' to the car!"

"Don't even tell me stories like that!" Thea said, waddling off to change her clothes, ignoring the men's laughter behind her. Turkeys.

She made it as far as the baby's room. A room she now entered with hope and anticipation instead of trepidation. The beautiful cradle was already set up in their bedroom—on Johnny's side of the bed, at his insistence—but she'd finally caved to the siren call of Babies "R" Us, so now there was a crib and a matching changing table and dresser, and a rocking chair, and an adorable bedding set in a bright blue plaid, in a room painted the color of French vanilla ice cream.

Thea hadn't even realized she was sitting cross-legged in the middle of the thick, blue-and-yellow checkerboard rug until she heard "You do realize you'll never get up from there, don't you?" behind her.

"Then I'll just wait here until the baby comes out."

Johnny's chuckle warmed her all the way through, making her think that their relationship was like one of her painted pieces before she varnished it—it looked okay, and it was usable enough, but the varnish not only made the colors richer, it protected it, too. That love was the varnish that protected a marriage, made it richer and deeper and—

Yeesh. Schmaltzy, much?

"I've been meaning to ask you," she said, watching Johnny gently shove the back of the rocking chair, "why's the house so big when it was just Andy and his wife?"

Johnny lowered himself into the chair, one leg extended close enough for Thea to touch his worn boot, if she'd wanted. "They apparently built the house expecting to fill it with kids. It just never happened."

"Oh. That's so sad."

"He and Maria adjusted. Her sisters had plenty of children, so there were always nieces and nephews around."

"And then he adopted you."

Johnny stared at her a long moment before more of a smirk than a smile stretched his lips. "Not that I was any prize."

"Oh, *stop,*" Thea said, playfully smacking the top of his boot, pretending she didn't hear the sourness curdling his words. Smartly moving the conversation along before it degenerated into yet another futile argument, she said, "So was this Rach's room when she was a baby?"

"No. By six weeks Kat moved her into the room down the hall."

"You're kidding? Why so far away?"

"You'd have to ask Kat that." He rubbed his mouth. "And I didn't feel in any position to argue. Even though I couldn't sleep right for months, worried the baby'd wake up and I wouldn't hear her. Half the time I'd end up bunking in the room next door, for my own peace of mind." He shrugged. "Except Rach slept like the dead for eleven hours every night from six weeks on."

"Which means odds are this one won't."

"Probably not."

Carefully, Thea said, "It must've killed you when Kat took Rach away."

Something flashed in his eyes before he got up and walked over to the crib. "I got over it," he said stiffly, then added, "although I sure didn't argue when Rach said she wanted to come back here to live with me instead of her mother." Thea watched, holding her breath, as he skimmed his hand over the smooth, arched top of the crib, then grasped it. "I guess I'd just hoped to have a little longer with her. That she wouldn't leave me again quite so soon."

Knowing how rare, and fragile, his candor was, Thea was afraid to speak. Almost. "Rach would have gone off to college, anyway," she said gently. "So she would've still left. At least this way she's just a couple hundred feet away."

"Yeah. With her *husband.*"

Honestly, she thought, trying to get up, but she would have had a better chance of flying. Johnny's lips curved.

"Change your mind about staying there until the kid's out?"

If nothing else, at least she was good for comic relief. "Gotta pee. But my center of gravity's clearly shifted to another county."

A second later Johnny squatted behind her to unceremoniously hoist her upright. Thea turned, looping her arms around his waist. "You think Rach doesn't need you anymore?"

Gently, he unwound her from his rib cage. "Got some paperwork in the office to tend to. You okay on your own for a while?"

"And I lived by myself for how long?" she said, thinking, *Wow, nice dodge.* "I think I can manage without your company for a few hours."

Smiling slightly, Johnny looked up at the walls. "You know…I'm thinking it's way too dull in here." His gaze dropped back to hers. "Maybe you could do something about that?"

Thea watched him leave, wondering how she'd managed to fall in love with the weirdest man on the planet.

Chapter Twelve

By the end of September, a herd of cheerful dinosaurs marched across the bottom half of one of the nursery walls and summer had given up the good fight. As had Thea, who'd reached that stage of pregnancy where she fit in *nothing,* she got winded walking from the living room to the kitchen and she could no longer reach the pedals in her car without the steering wheel gouging her stomach.

In other words, her life was reduced to waiting, worrying and watching TV, not necessarily in that order. All those years she'd prayed to carry a baby to term; now all she wanted was to *get this damn thing out* already.

"One more week until the magic thirty-seven," Naomi said, hefting Thea upright on the exam table. "Then little Whosits won't be premature. You might want to take a break from sex until then, just to be on the safe side."

Thea gave her a you-gotta-be-kidding-me look. "Like I'm gonna feel more like it when I'm even bigger?"

The doctor helped Thea down off the table. Then guided her feet into the Crocs she couldn't see. "Some women do."

"Bully for them," Thea said as she clumsily lowered herself into the chair in front of Naomi's desk.

"Johnny couldn't come with you today?"

"Out-of-town buyers," Thea said with a shrug. "It happens."

"But things are otherwise okay between you?"

She would bring that up. "The cranky pregnant lady hasn't scared Johnny off yet, so I guess that's good, right?"

"And?"

Thea sighed. "I'm trying, Naomi. I really am. But..." Her eyes burned. "How the hell am I supposed to connect with somebody who doesn't want to?"

"Doesn't want to? Or is afraid to?"

Her mouth pulled tight, Thea looked out the office's single window, thinking of the aborted conversations that passed for communication these days. The constant apology in Johnny's eyes that invariably accompanied them. "Does it matter," she said, struggling to her feet, "if the outcome's the same?"

Before she could get away, Naomi put her hands on her shoulders. "And did it ever occur to you that the man's in love?" she said quietly, and Thea's eyes popped open.

"And here I thought you wanted me to hold this baby in for another week! Geez. Naomi—you been smoking something between appointments?"

The doctor laughed. "I'm serious. And so's Johnny. He's not holding back because he doesn't love you, he's holding back because he *does*."

"You do realize that makes no sense whatsoever?"

"Love never does. But Pop tells me things. So does Rachel. And I see the way he looks at you, like he's scared to death—"

"Naomi? Not helping."

The doctor smiled. "Not of you. Exactly. Of what you represent."

"What the heck is that supposed to mean?"

Still smiling, Naomi walked her to the door, pulled it open. "Just don't write him off quite yet, okay?"

Like there was any chance of that, Thea thought some hours later, watching Johnny—get this—toss a ball out front for J.D. and Chuck, laughing his ass off when the pair of 'em kept colliding as they dove for the ball at the same time.

Dude was gonna drive her insane.

"If you're not careful," she called out from the porch where she was sitting on one of the rocking chairs, all wrapped up in the couch throw, "the dogs're gonna end up liking you more than they do me."

He tossed the ball again. "Guess I better start being mean to 'em, then. Well, don't just stand there, mutt," he said when Chuck got the ball and J.D. looked back, bereft. Johnny circled his hand. "Show your *cojones* and go get it from him!"

"You forget," Thea said. "*Cojones* are kind of in short supply in that lot."

"J.D. knows what I mean. Doncha, boy?" With a joyful *rowlf!* J.D. charged Chuck and snatched the ball away from him. Imagine that.

"Can't wait to see you play catch with our little guy," Thea said, holding her breath. Mentally keeping an eye out in case the ugly little dude who lived in Johnny's brain made a sudden reappearance, like it was prone to do. When Johnny said, "Me, too," she relaxed, a little. The temperature dipping with the sun, she snuggled more deeply into the throw. Tiptoed a little further out into the conversation. "I wonder if he'll be blond or dark haired."

"Long as he's not a redhead, I'm good."

"What's wrong with redheads?"

"You got any on your side?"

"Not to my knowledge."

"Neither do I," Johnny said, aiming a grin in her direction, and Thea thought about what Naomi had said and her heart did a double somersault. Because at moments like this, she could almost believe in miracles.

Her heart tight in her chest, she said, "And you've got some nerve provoking me when you know I can't come after you!" Johnny's laughter encouraged her to venture out another inch or so. "I s'pose we really do need to get serious about naming this kid. Obviously both our fathers' names are out—"

"Obviously," Johnny said, yanking the ball out of J.D.'s slobbery mouth.

"And there's no names on my mother's side I'd even consider. Not taking anything away from my grandfather, but I'm not naming my kid Wilbur."

"Good call."

Thea smiled. "Any names in your mother's family we might consider?"

Silence. The brand of silence Thea'd come to dread over the past few months. No surprise then, when he said in a clipped tone, "I was never close to any of 'em. Why would I want to use one of their names for my son?"

Once again feeling defeated, she stood. "Fine. But if we don't come up with something soon the kid's gonna be answering to 'Hey, you.'" Hearing the edge to her voice, she said, more softly, "Supper's probably ready by now. May as well go inside."

"Meat loaf's good," Johnny said, breaking the uncustomary silence. Usually they did a pretty good job of keeping the conversation going, acting like a normal couple, whatever the hell that meant.

But every day, it was getting harder. Harder to pretend. To hang on to his control. To dodge Thea's amazing knack for hitting the sore spot, over and over…

"Thanks," she said, barely looking at him. Thea didn't mope or act the drama queen, ever—Rach had that crown sewed up tight—she'd just go flat, like old soda. And Johnny felt like crap, knowing it was his fault.

Par for the course, right?

"What do you think of maybe naming the baby Andy?" he said, his fork hovering over his plate. Thea looked up, the space between her brows creased. "Since he never had kids of his own and all."

Her eyes softened in that way that twisted him up inside, sucking him in deeper. Why couldn't he have inherited the heartless bastard gene along with his father's crooked bottom teeth and square chin? Better yet, why hadn't Thea's experiences left her bitter and whiny, instead of resilient and generous and loving?

"I think that's a great idea. Andrew Griego," she said, smiling. "I like it."

"It was actually Andres, but Andrew works."

"Andres is fine, if you'd like to keep the Latino heritage thing going. Oh! Then maybe we could use your mother's maiden name as his second name. Santiago, right?"

"How the hell did you know that?"

"From her obit, maybe? Andres Santiago Griego. I really like that—"

"No way are we using my mother's name," Johnny said quietly, forking in a bite of potatoes.

A moment's silence preceded, "Care to clue me in as to why not?"

"Personal reasons," he said, hearing himself. Hating himself.

Hating that trying to fix things kept leading back down this same damn road, for reasons he couldn't begin to figure out.

Several seconds passed before Thea wordlessly got up to carry her still-full plate to the sink.

"I can get that—"

"I'm pregnant, not helpless," she said, sharply enough to make more than one dog think twice about begging for the scraps.

"Dammit, Thea, don't do this."

The dish still in her hands, Thea clumsily wheeled around, sending chunks of uneaten meat loaf and potatoes flying directly into waiting dogs' mouths. "You know, I can deal with you saying you don't love me," she said, making him cringe. "But why can't you at least trust me?"

"Are you kidding me? I've never trusted anybody the way I trust you!"

The plate set on the counter, Thea crossed her arms over her belly. "Oh, right. For weeks I've been walking on eggshells around you, afraid I'll say something to send you into one of your funks. But the worst part of it is, I don't even know where I'm not supposed to go, because you won't talk to me!"

"That's nuts, we talk all the damn time—"

"Not about the important stuff. Not about whatever's keeping you from believing you're…you're *worthy* of being loved!"

Over the ringing in his ears—and wondering how on earth Thea'd made that particular leap—Johnny said, "You shouldn't be getting so worked up, it's not good for you or the baby—"

"And you will so not play the little-woman's-too-pregnant card with me, buster!" She got right up in his face, eyes blazing, and Johnny felt every cell in his body catch fire. "Maybe I gave you the benefit of the doubt at first, that you were just protecting a broken heart and all. Only after living with you these past weeks, I don't buy it."

"Why would it be anything else?"

"Because the pieces don't fit, Johnny! You seek me out, you hold me when we sleep, you put an extra cover on me when you leave in the morning, for God's sake—"

"I'm just taking care of you!" he said, feeling hot and shaky, like a volcano about to erupt.

She grunted out a laugh. "Nobody, including my own mother, takes care of me like you do! For somebody with a broken heart, you sure as hell put yourself out there. But only so far. Because the minute I cross some invisible line you've laid down…bam! The door slams in my face. So I'm thinking this isn't about you not being able to love me. It's that you won't let me love *you*."

Johnny's throat knotted. "You knew what the deal was going in. And at least I was honest—"

"But that's just it, you weren't. Not then, and not now. It's like I see you tottering on the brink of something real, but over and over, you pull back. And that *hurts,* you bozo. Because I thought I could at least count on you to be open with me—"

"And maybe you have to trust *me,*" Johnny ground out, "that whatever's going on in my head has nothing to do with you."

For several seconds she simply stared at him, tears bulging in her eyes, then trundled away, calling the dogs after her.

After the debacle in the kitchen, Thea and Company wandered into Maria's prissy little parlor, thinking to drown her sorrows in the pages of a yellowing, glitz-and-glamour '70s paperback. Except after several minutes of all the stomping about and door slamming going on in other parts of the house, she realized she'd read the same page a half dozen times and still had no idea what was going on.

Must. Get. Out. Of. House.

Righty-o, she thought, closing the door behind her and the

dogs. Couldn't walk, wasn't much inclined to drive, and who could she possibly dump on, anyway? Tess or Winnie? Rachel? Her *mother?*

Yeah, that'd work.

Thea stood in the clearing between the house and the barns, her breath coming in short, frustrated pants. *And people wonder why I'm cynical,* she thought, her lip actually curling. But over the frustration, a voiceless urging to be still. To listen. Almost angrily, she tilted back her head, watching the stars pop into view in the wedges of plum-colored sky visible through the shuddering, rustling trees.

Fine, You want me to listen, I'm listening, because for damn sure I've run out of ideas—

The sound of the barn door shutting startled her; squinting, she made out Carlos's hunched silhouette hobbling in her direction.

"That you, Miss Thea?"

"Nobody else."

"Huh," he said, coming close enough to see her in the soupy light from the security fixture over the barn. "Mus' be the night for bad moods. Firs' Mr. Johnny, then you... You two have a fight?"

"Sort of." Hugging herself, Thea looked back up at the stars. "Why's he so sad, Carlos?"

"You think Mr. Johnny's sad?"

"Not think. Know. Oh, he hides it well enough, but it's always there, just below the surface. Or am I the only one who sees it?"

"No," the old ranch hand said after a long moment. "You're not. Don' think many other people do, though."

"I'm his *wife,* Carlos," she said, her eyes filling. "More important, I'm his *friend.* And it's making me crazy—*he's* making me crazy—because he won't let me help. Or at least try. It's like...like there's something poisonous inside him that needs to come out. But instead of letting it, he just keeps swallowing it back down."

"It's getting cold," Carlos said after a pause. "Why don' you come inside, I'll make you a cup of nice, hot tea?"

"Oh…no, that's okay. I just needed to vent for a moment—"

"Please."

And along with the single word, an imploring gaze she couldn't ignore. Or refuse. Sucking in a breath, she nodded, then slowly climbed the stairs to the old man's tidy little apartment over the barn, the twin bed tightly made with a plain, dark green blanket, the small wooden table and chairs in the rudimentary kitchen sparkling clean. Carlos gestured toward the single, worn upholstered chair, waiting until she was seated before asking, "You know how Johnny came to work for Mr. Andy?"

"Just what Johnny told me, that he and Andy'd sometimes see each other in town, that eventually he offered him an after-school job. Why?"

A blue-tinged flame whooshed to life underneath the old-fashioned kettle squatting on a small gas range. "You don' remember him from that time, I take it?"

"He started working here when he was fourteen, right? I would've only been nine. So no. Not really."

Carlos pulled a lone mug from the drainboard by the sink. "To tell you the truth," he said, wiping it with a dish towel, "when Johnny firs' come out here? None of us hands liked him much. Kid had a bug up his butt size of Texas. Snarled instead of talked, when he said anythin' at all. But he was a hard worker, and a fas' learner, and little by little Mr. Andy somehow started wearing down his rough edges. Mos' important, Johnny took to the horses right away. Mr. Andy, he wouldn't never let nobody lay a hand on 'em, an' Johnny, too—it was like somethin' magic would come over him when he was aroun' them."

The kettle whistled; as Thea idly watched Carlos pour the steaming water over a teabag in the mug, she thought of Johnny's tenderness and patience with the horses. The same tenderness and patience he showed her, come to think of it. When she wasn't nagging him about being open with her, that is.

"Sugar?" Carlos asked, unaware of the mix of exasperation and shame tingling Thea's face.

"Thank you, yes."

"One or two?"

"Three."

A minute later, Carlos handed her the mug, then pulled out the nearest kitchen chair and sat, palms planted on his spread thighs.

"Okay. I never tol' anybody this before, except for Mr. Andy. But one day, maybe a year after Johnny comes to work for Mr. Andy? He sends me and Johnny up to the north pasture to repair some fencing. An' oh, my Lord, it's hot. The sun's beating down on us, you know? And Johnny—he was a scrawny kid, small for his age—he looks like he's gonna melt. So I take off my shirt, and I tell Johnny, it's okay, go ahead. But at firs' he wouldn't. Finally, though, he does. And *Dios mio*..." Carlos shook his head. "I don' know if I should say something, or preten' like I don' notice or what—"

"Notice what?"

"The welts, *querida*," he said, and her heart stopped. "Right across his back, maybe ten, twelve of 'em. I'm telling you, somebody had beat that poor kid, but good. An' it wasn't his father, because that man had already been gone three, four years, by that point."

"Oh, dear God...what did Johnny say?"

"When he sees me staring, he grabs his shirt and puts it

back on, real fast, giving me this look like maybe I should think twice before sayin' anything. But that night, after the kid goes back home? I tell Mr. Andy and Miz Maria. An' oh, my, you shoulda seen Mr. Andy's face. I never, ever see him that mad before.

"The nex' day, I'm bringing one of the mares back to the barn and I hear this loud argument, you know? Johnny and his mother, only it's his mother doing most of the yelling. So I put two and two together, I'm thinking Mr. Andy must've said something to Johnny's mother, an' that she didn' take it so good. There she is, lighting into him like you wouldn' believe, saying he's not worth nothing, why he always has to go aroun' causing trouble for her, how she wished he'd never been born. Things no mother should ever be saying, even thinking, about her own child."

"D-did you stop her?" Thea said over her trembling.

"Before I could, there's Mr. Andy—he apparently heard the whole thing—tellin' the *bruha,* she don' want the boy, don' appreciate him, Mr. Andy'd be happy to give him a home. An' jus' like that, she lets him go. Walks away with her hands up in the air like this—" he lifted his own hands in a gesture of surrender "—saying somethin' about how Johnny wasn't her problem no more."

When Thea found her voice, she said, "Johnny said he came to live here after his mother died."

"That's when Mr. Andy and *la señora* adopted him for good, when Johnny was sixteen. But he was living here for a good year before that. Maybe longer, I don' really remember."

Her emotions hopelessly snarled, Thea shook her head. "He never said a word."

"There's two kinds of men, *querida,*" Carlos said gently. "The ones who can't forget the past, an' the ones who preten' it never happened. An' Mr. Johnny, he don' want nobody feeling sorry for him. After all these years, he still don' know I saw his mama and him that day. Or that—a couple months after that—I caught him crying his eyes out behind the mares' barn."

"Oh, Carlos…no. What did you do?"

"*Nada.* An' don't look at me like that, Johnny didn' want nobody comforting him."

"And you knew this how? For God's sake—he was still a *kid!* Why would you assume he didn't want somebody to talk to?"

A half smile curved the old man's lips. "See, that's the difference between men and women. Maybe we bury our pain, or maybe we act on it, we but we don' talk about it much. We think—" he shrugged "—what's the point? An' Johnny's always struck me as jus' one of those people who's gotta be left alone to lick his own wounds."

Ain't that the truth? Thea thought on a released breath, even as, slowly, a few more pieces of the puzzle that was Johnny Griego fell into place. One hand clamped on the chair arm, she pushed herself to her feet, setting her empty cup on the bare table. "You really haven't told a soul about any of this, not once in twenty-five years?"

"No. Nobody."

"Not even Rachel's mother?"

One corner of the old man's mouth lifted. "Especially not her."

"Then why me? Why now?"

Now on his feet as well, Carlos folded his arms across his barrel chest. "Because you understan' something about Mr. Johnny that nobody else ever did—that jus' because he's pretending the past never happened, that don' mean he ever forgot about it."

Thea's mouth stretched tight. "*Touché,* as the kids say. So now what?"

It was a rhetorical question, but Carlos answered anyway.

"Every day for twenty-five years, I see those shadows in his eyes. An' I see the love in yours. More love than I see in anybody else's, except for maybe his daughter. So I think…maybe that love is strong enough to erase those shadows, no?"

"Oh, Carlos," Thea said on a sigh. "I don't know. Sometimes I think he's grown quite partial to those shadows." She cocked her head. "If you don't want me to say anything to Johnny—"

"An' if I didn' expect you to make good use of the information," Carlos said, a grin spreading across his creased cheeks, "I would've kept my big mouth shut, yes?"

Except the question was, she thought as turned toward the door leading to the outside stairs, what was she supposed to do with the information? Understanding why Johnny went weird on her every time she mentioned his mother was one thing, confronting him directly about it something else altogether—

"No, don' go that way," Carlos said, "go down through the barn, there's no light out back, you might trip." When she balked, he chuckled. "The horses, they're all locked up good an' tight, *querida,* you'll be fine."

Apparently word of her irrational fear of the livestock had gotten around. Great.

"You wan' me to go with you?" the old man said.

"Of course not. Don't be ridiculous."

And actually, as she trudged through the dimly lit barn most of the residents couldn't have been less interested in her presence, although one or two mares seemed mildly curious whuffling softly as she passed, like friendly neighbors just saying, "Hey."

Except for the newest addition, a gentle, dreamy-eyed dapple gray Aidan had recently bought for Winnie, which—along with his other two horses—boarded with Johnny. As Thea got closer, the big animal hung her head over the stall gate, nodding at her and snorting—the horse version of "Pssst."

And what business did she have demanding that Johnny face his fears if she wasn't willing to do the same?

Holding her breath—not from the smell, but from sheer terror—Thea inched closer, until the horse dipped her beautiful, massive head to gently nudge Thea's shoulder. Sighing out her anxiety, Thea lifted one hand to stroke the velvety nose, so absorbed in bonding with her new friend she hardly registered the barn door opening.

Johnny stood stock-still, watching, wondering why he'd never bothered to ask Thea why she was afraid of horses. Although, judging from her giggles as the horse started nibbling her hair, he supposed it was a moot point now.

"She's looking for a treat," he said, and she whipped around—as best as she was able—her cheeks darkening.

"How long have you been standing there?"

"Long enough," he said as he walked toward her, forcing himself back inside the spinning, mind-blowing vortex that was Thea. "I got worried, when I couldn't find you."

Her cheek pressed to the horse's snout, she almost smiled. "And where would I have gone?"

"Fear's got nothing to do with logic."

She pulled away from the mare, patting her neck. "That's certainly true."

Johnny pressed a hand into the rock-hard muscles at the base of his skull. "You been in here the whole time?"

Thea nodded toward the ceiling. "Carlos and I were having a chat. Over tea."

"What about?"

"Just stuff. Old times on the ranch, mostly."

For once, Johnny couldn't read her expression, and it was driving him nuts. He felt like he should apologize. But for what? Being himself? *Protecting* himself?

He shoved back his denim jacket to slide his fingers into his jeans' pockets. "You still mad?"

She took forever to answer. "No," she finally said.

A stinging sensation started up at the back of his throat. "I don't want to hurt you, Thea. I really don't."

Her lips curving, she moved into his arms and held on tight, her lack of response making him uneasy as all hell.

Thirteen

"Holy moley," Thea said as Johnny lugged the last of the baby rap she'd scored at her shower from his truck into the nursery. We'll have to have three more kids just to use all of this up."

Having apparently hijacked the shower from Tess, Evanelista had then invited everyone who'd ever eaten in the iner. As in, the entire town. And they'd all come. Bearing ifts. Many, many gifts.

Over yet another when-is-this-damn-shoe-gonna-drop-ready? prickle of apprehension—at least the hundredth in e past two weeks—Johnny chuckled at the four mega boxes f disposable diapers taking up half the room.

"Those oughta last us a couple of weeks. Maybe," he said, owning when Thea dumped a small mountain of baby othes off the rocker and sank into it, hugely bellied and even ore hugely miserable.

"You okay?"

"Other than thinking another two weeks of this and I migh kill myself, I'm just peachy."

"Hmm. Well…you're in the safe zone now. We could—'

"And you can stop that thought right there. Don't take thi personally, but I'd rather gouge my eyes out with a spoon tha have sex right now. In fact, I'm seriously thinking of neve having sex again. Ever."

Naomi had warned him that the closer Thea got to deliver the crankier she'd probably get. Rate she was going she'd hav this baby in the next ten minutes.

But at least she was too focused on the baby—and he misery—to go back down certain roads she'd been so deter mined to travel a few weeks earlier, even if he strongly sus pected the reprieve was only temporary, that sooner or late she'd remember that bone she'd buried and go digging it u again to wave it in his face. What would happen then he ha no idea. Because there was a difference between working a marriage and trying too hard to make it work.

Unfortunately, he suspected they both knew which of thos more nearly described their situation.

"Come on," he said, prying her out of the chair. "I'll mak a fire in the family room, you do the blimp thing on the so while I reheat the leftover stew for supper." The weather ha turned sharply colder in the last few hours, bypassing fall a together and crashing right into winter. There'd even bee snow clouds, last time he was outside. Gotta love October i the mountains, where you could swim and ski on the sam day, if conditions were right.

Thea sighed. "You mind if the blimp eats on the sofa?"

"Not a bit."

Sure enough, while Johnny was nuking the stew Ozzie made the day before, it started to snow, piddly little flakes l doubted would amount to more than a dusting. Still, when l returned to the family room with their suppers and saw the pained looked on Thea's face, worry spiked.

"Everything okay?"

"Just thinking," she said, taking the bowl from him. Her feet up, her back propped against the couch's arm, she balanced the bowl on her belly to eat, grousing when the baby kicked and made her jerk. Johnny handed her several extra paper napkins, then sat across from her.

"What about?" he asked, offhandedly, only to feel his blood freeze when her gaze lanced his and he realized she'd never buried the bone, after all. That she'd kept it right in her sights the whole time. Outside, the snow picked up the pace, ticking nervously against the windows.

"How come you never told me about the way your mother treated you?"

Gentle as her voice was, the words sliced like shattered glass. Unable to eat, Johnny set his bowl on a side table, glowering at the trio of hopeful dogs at his knees. "I have no idea what you're talking about—"

"The night I talked to Carlos? He told me about that day she came up here looking for you. After…after he'd seen the welts on your back. The things she said to you. That when Andy intervened…" Her eyes glistened. "That she basically gave you away, like a dog she'd grown tired of."

Breathe, man. Breathe.

"How in God's name did Carlos know about that?"

The sympathy in her eyes lacerated his heart. "By being in the wrong place at the right time. He also swears he never said a word to anybody, about any of it."

"Until you."

Her gaze was unflinching. "Yeah. Because like Rachel, like me, he's worried about you. Worried you've kept all this crap locked up inside you for too damn long—"

"And it still doesn't concern you," Johnny snapped, on his feet and striding to the window, heart and mind racing, from her, the memories, all of it—

"Hey!" Thea said, her voice yanking him back. "In case you missed it, bucko, we're about to have a child together! So you'd better believe that anything that might affect our baby concerns me!"

"And why the hell should something that happened twenty-five years ago have any impact on our kid?"

"Because it's still impacting you, ya dumb cluck!"

Johnny glared at Thea for several seconds before finally tearing his gaze from hers. The snow was getting heavier, like it meant business. "Preferring to let the past stay there isn't a fault."

"It is if you haven't dealt with it."

"I dealt with it just fine!" he said, wheeling on her. "I put it all behind me and got on with my life, and for damn sure I don't need anybody's pity over something I've spent the better part of my life trying to forget! And I couldn't have stood that having Kat pity me—"

He jerked around again, his heart thundering.

"Why?" Thea said softly behind him. "Because she was *perfect?* Got news for you, buddy—more than once I caught her in the girls' bathroom, tossing her cookies before she took a test—"

"I meant to say you," Johnny lied. "I don't want *your* pity."

"Then it's all good, because you don't have it." She paused. "In case you haven't figured it out yet, babe, I'm not Kat. My heart can break for you without pitying you, okay? Because when you love somebody, you ache for them when they hurt. Even if that hurt was a long time ago." A beat or two passed before she added, "Even if they don't tell you what that hurt is."

"And why can't you just leave it be, Thea?" Johnny said on a weary sigh. "Why can't you leave *me* be? I swear to you I won't let it affect our son—"

"And ignoring your feelings doesn't make them any less real," Thea said with unnerving calmness. "Believe me, I know whereof I speak." She paused. "Or have you forgotten how pissed you were about me being scared to go to the doctor? Or about how scared I was about anything to do with the baby, for that matter. You weren't about to let me hide behind my fears, Johnny. I'm just returning the favor. Now, you don't want to talk to me, that's fine. But you need to talk to somebody. Because the longer you ignore the garbage, the worse it stinks."

Knowing they could continue this argument until the cows came home and get nowhere, Johnny frowned out the window; between the deepening dusk and the much heavier snow, he could barely see the barn. A few seconds later, Thea said, "Looks pretty bad out there. You'd better see to the horses before it gets any worse."

There was irony for you, Johnny thought sourly, that Thea was easing into her role as rancher's wife even as her role as *his* wife was becoming less defined by the second.

Slowly, he faced her, recoiling at the love and pain and determination in her eyes, his gut churning with the old futility of knowing his apology was worthless.

His eyes lowered, he headed out of the room. "I won't be long."

"Take your time. It's not like I'm going anywhere."

He turned. "You sure of that?"

"Go," she said quietly, stroking Norma Jean's silky head, the yellow dog's chin nestled atop their unborn son, and Johnny's jaw clenched in frustration, that the damn dogs knew how to love Thea better than he did.

* * *

Thinking *Well, then. Now you know,* Thea felt the house's shudder as Johnny yanked shut the back door. And yet her heart still twanged as, her gaze fixed on the picture window facing the barn, she watched him trudge through the swirling snow, bowed slightly from the weight of all that responsibility.

"Oh, Johnny," she whispered, shifting to ease the near constant ache in her lower back, "what am I gonna do with you? About you?"

She couldn't decide which was worse—the idea of spending the rest of her life avoiding the apology in those dark eyes, or of leaving him alone, a thought that made her heart squeeze so tight she could hardly breathe.

Speaking of squeezing…the baby shoved his head into her bladder so hard she saw stars.

Her painfully full bladder.

Grumbling, Thea pushed herself to her feet, barely clearing the antique rug before she peed all over herself.

"Holy crap," she muttered to the scattered, thoroughly confused dogs, only to gasp when the first contraction hit, like a blowtorch to her crotch, and Thea let loose with a string of cuss words she'd apparently been saving up for just such an occasion. When the pain subsided, it occurred to her that Johnny often spent a good hour settling the horses down in the evening, and that, judging from the intensity of that first contraction, she might not *have* an hour. She grabbed the portable phone off the sofa table, dialing Johnny's cell with shaking hands. Heard his ringtone from the kitchen. Damn.

And Rach and Jess had gone to the movies. In Santa Fe.

Muttering, "It's gonna be fine, it's gonna be fine, it's gonna be fine," Thea inched soggily to the French doors, threw one open and said to the congregation of tilted heads in front of her, "Somebody, anybody—go get Johnny!"

Amazingly, Chuck actually approached the door, only to recoil from all the cold wet stuff flying into his face. He shook, then looked at Thea with a *You're not serious* expression.

"There's an eight-ounce sirloin in it for you if you do," she said, and the dog considered his options for a second, then launched himself into the storm, although for all she knew he was just going to take a whiz, and he'd be back in a second.

Thea let out a cackle of hysterical laughter, only to choke when the next contraction knocked the stuffing out of her.

"Arf!"

Startled, Johnny looked up from the feed bin to see a snow-dusted Chuck standing outside the open barn door, frantically pacing and running in circles.

"Chuck? What—"

"Arf! Arf!" The dog dashed inside, tugged at Johnny's gloved hand, then gallumphed back outside. Snow flew as the dog spun, landing with feet splayed and wild eyes, giving Johnny a *Dude! Get your ass in gear,* now! look.

Johnny's heart exploded, then settled into a head-rattling *whompwhompwhomp.* With fumbling hands he quickly latched closed Maggie's stall, shouting in the direction of the mariachi music coming from upstairs to keep an eye out, Thea was having the baby, even as it occurred to him he didn't actually know that's what was going on.

Except he did, he thought as he strode after the frantic dog, who kept running ahead, then back, then ahead again, like Johnny wasn't moving fast enough.

"Thea!" Johnny bellowed the instant he and the dog pushed through the back door, only to skid to a stop, sure his heartbeat was gonna take off the top of his skull. All wrapped up in her shawl, her hospital bag on the floor beside her, she was

pale and trembling and grinning so hard he thought her cheeks would crack, not to mention the brittle, fragile wall around his heart.

"You sent the dog?" he said.

She beamed even harder, although this time at Chuck, prancing around like somebody should give him a medal. "I promised him s-steak."

"Done," Johnny said, a moment before Thea grabbed for him, her face contorted, and he felt the bottom fall out of his stomach: she'd gone straight into hard labor.

"Good girl," he said when she was done, and Thea laughed and said, ruefully, "Ozzie's gonna kill me. There's a lake in the middle of the family room," and Johnny said, "Ozzie will get over it. How many of those have you had so far?"

"Enough to know it's not the meat loaf. I called Naomi. She said she'd meet us at the hospital." And Johnny thought, *Right. Snow. Not good.* "How's the snow?"

"Not that bad," he said, guiding her toward the door, grabbing his cell off the counter and stuffing it in his pocket. In clear weather it took twenty minutes to get the hospital. With the snow and her water already broken and her labor going lickety-split…

"You're thinking we won't make it, aren't you? And don't you dare lie to me."

Johnny opened the door. Man, it was *really* white out there.

"Oh, hell," Thea said. "Go ahead, lie."

"It's gonna be okay," he said, steering her outside. "Truck's got new tires, and I can drive in just about anything. So we're gonna get you to the hospital—"

"Where they have all those lovely drugs," she said, brightening. This from the woman who didn't take aspirin, for God's sake.

"Where they have all those lovely drugs—" he opened the passenger-side door and hefted her up into the seat "—and you're gonna have a baby, and everything's gonna be okay. I promise."

Johnny slammed shut her door and hotfooted it around to his side. "Well, then," Thea said when he got in, "I'm in your hands, bucko."

His mouth twitching, he rammed the key into the ignition. "No arguments?"

"Nary a one."

"Now's a helluva time to go putting your faith in me," he muttered, turning on the headlights. And glory hallelujah, he could see. More or less.

"I think this is called working with what you've got," Thea said, her breath hitching as another contraction hit. "Just don't…forget…the drugs," she panted as Johnny put the truck into gear and inched forward, the snowflakes assaulting the headlight beams like a swarm of angry white locusts.

Thea had no idea how long it took them to reach the road leading into town from Johnny's ranch, but *forever* came close.

Don't freak, don't freak, don't—

"You okay over there?" Johnny said.

"Sure thing," she muttered, shutting her eyes against the whiteout, the panic, the pain.

"It's okay if you moan or whatever. It won't bother me," Johnny said, and she might have been tempted to laugh if she hadn't felt like she was being ripped in two.

"Yeah, I seem to remember that," she got out, moments before the blowtorch did its thing again, and Johnny reached over to massage her shoulder and she nearly lost it.

"You keep both hands on that wheel, you hear me?"

"Yes, ma'am," he said, removing his hand. Then he added,

"It's gonna be okay, honey. Worse comes to worse, I can deliver this baby."

"You got drugs on you?"

"Well, no, but—"

"Then you are so not delivering this baby. Holy crud…the pain's getting really strong now."

"It's probably not as bad as you think, you've just never felt it before."

She clamped a hand around his arm and hissed, between gasps for oxygen, "And the only reason…I'm letting you live…is because you're currently…my only means of scoring an…epidural."

"Sorry," he said, and she thought, *Suuure, you are,* and then he suggested maybe she'd feel better if she called Naomi, and Thea said, yeah, she'd do that, just as soon as she unhooked her hands from *around his neck.*

She might have yelled that last part.

A moment later she heard, "Yeah, we're on our way. The snow seems to be easing up. Hopefully it'll be smooth sailing from now on." He turned to Thea. "Naomi's already at the hospital, soon as you get there everything's good to go—"

Thea let loose with another round of reeeally colorful cuss words.

"Honey?" she heard Naomi say, vaguely registering that Johnny had put his phone on speaker mode. "Okay, talk to me while Johnny drives. Is there still space between the contractions or are they coming right on top of each other?"

"That last thing," she said through a grimace, gripping the dashboard. "Omigod, this can't be right, it hurts so damn *much…*"

"I know it hurts, sweetie, but it's not hurting *you,* I promise. Or the baby. Last time we checked, he was in perfect position, ready to pop right out, so it's all good, okay?" Then, through another wave of pain, she heard something about "she's in transition" and "might not make it that far" and Johnny's saying they were just about there, could she hang on for fifteen more minutes?

Thea shrieked as a sensation like trying to poop out a watermelon knocked the breath right out of her.

"You feel like pushing?" came Naomi's voice through the phone.

"Oh…my…*Gaaahhhhd!*"

"I'll take that as a yes," Johnny said.

"Then she's not going to make it," Thea heard, clear as a bell, because, bizarrely, the pain had suddenly backed off. "Is there someplace you can go, because it might be better if you don't have to deliver the baby in the truck—"

"I'll second that," Thea said, afraid to breathe.

"Got it covered," Johnny said, pulling over. When she realized where they were, she nearly laughed, except the next urge to push rushed through her like a flooded arroyo after a cloudburst. A second later Johnny was tugging her out of the truck and up into his arms, carting her toward the place where, as it happened, little Mr. No Name had been conceived.

"I must weigh a ton," she said into his chest.

"I've lifted heavier," he said, all gentleness and concentration of purpose.

Thea looked up into his grim expression, barely visible in the weird, pinkish light and she thought, *I'd be a fool to leave this man.* The snow had stopped, the moon peeking through the tattered, empty clouds. "I'm sorry," she said, and his gaze dropped to hers.

"Yeah," he said, setting her down in two inches of powder long enough to unearth her spare key from where she kept it underneath a snow-crusted planter. "It was real inconsiderate of you to go into labor during a snowstorm." The door unlocked, he swept her up into his arms again and shouldered his way inside. "We'll have to have a serious talk about that—" he kicked the door shut with his foot "—someday."

The next several seconds were a blur of lights and heat going on, Johnny's stripping the bed with a single motion, his gently tugging off her maternity jeans and settling her back against a bunch of pillows. From her bathroom he brought towels and her vinyl shower curtain; from God knows where he unearthed some thread and a pair of scissors.

"You act like you actually know what you're doing."

"It's not a bed of straw, but it'll do. Naomi's called the EMTs and she's on her way, but there's no telling if any of them'll make it in time." Expressionless, he tugged off her panties, spread the shower curtain and a couple towels underneath her.

"You scared?" she whispered.

Over a slight, bemused smile, his gaze touched hers. "You're the one having this baby. I'm just here to catch."

"You didn't answer my question."

"And I'm not gonna. Although let's just say I'm real glad I paid close attention when Rach was born."

"That was eighteen years ago!"

"And every detail's indelibly etched into my brain, trust me."

Like I've got a choice? she thought as another urge to push curled her forward, bearing down, helping her baby out, while Johnny did the cheerleading thing from the other side of her knees. Which he kept up for the next heaven-knows-how-long, it wasn't like she was looking at a clock, for heaven's sake, until—

"Nearly over, babe, I can see the head!"

"Are you sure?"

He gave her a look. "Yeah. I'm sure. You should see all the black hair!"

"That's—"

"No, it's not. You're a blonde, remember?"

Thea actually laughed, too, then clutched the covers to push again, crying out against the burn as the baby stretched her, and she heard Johnny say, "One more push, honey," like he'd been delivering babies his whole life—hoofless ones, anyway—and she did, gasping in sudden relief a second later, almost too stunned to register Johnny's, "Head's out, no cord around his neck, we're good, aaaaand…here he is!" Moments later, the baby cradled in his arms, Johnny looked over at her, tears shining in his eyes. "He's perfect, honey," he whispered. "He's absolutely perfect."

"Gimme," she said, holding out her arms, and Johnny gently laid the messy, squirming baby on Thea's tummy, covering him with another towel and rubbing him all over—"Pretty much like we do with the foals," he said, making her sputter another laugh—and then the baby let out a squeak, then a squawk, at being so rudely expelled from his nice, warm bed.

"Omigod," Thea whispered, sniffling, touching her baby's soft, soft cheek with her fingertip. "Hey, sweetheart. It's your m-mommy," she said, dissolving into tears a split second before Johnny wrapped them both up in his arms, tucking Thea's head beneath his chin. And even in the tsunami of emotions following the birth, Thea felt something shift. Startled, she looked into Johnny's eyes, her heart stumbling, then righting, when she saw what she'd been waiting and hoping and praying for her entire adult life—

"And you couldn't have waited *five* more minutes!" came from the doorway.

A deliriously happy Thea grinned up at Naomi, fast-tracking toward the bed. "Come see! Isn't he *gorgeous?*"

"Oh, my…isn't he just," the doctor said, smiling as she carefully unwrapped the towel to check the baby out. Moments later, the cord efficiently tied and cut, she lifted the tiny bundle into Johnny's arms. "Okay, Daddy…you take Junior here for a few minutes so I can tend to Mama."

About an inch away from overwhelmed, Johnny carried the bundled baby out to the living area, settling into a corner of Thea's striped sofa. "Hey, little guy," he whispered, his eyes stinging even as he smiled. "Somebody's been waiting a long time to meet you."

And not just Thea.

Not that he hadn't fallen in love with Rachel every bit as hard as he had for this tiny, mop-headed little boy. It was just different, with a boy.

The obligation, however, was the same. Not just to the child, but—he glanced over at Thea, fussing at Naomi's fussing over her as she talked to Rachel on her cell, and he glowed inside with what he could no longer deny—but to the child's mother. With that, he finally got back around to what he'd been thinking before Chuck had sounded the alarm, about how, when he'd stepped up to the plate for Kat after she'd told him she was pregnant, there'd been nothing conditional about it, nothing half-assed. On his part, anyway. Maybe he hadn't known jack-squat about being a husband, but all the same he'd gone into it completely committed. That Kat's commitment hadn't matched his wasn't really anybody's fault.

Especially not Thea's, who didn't deserve to pay the price for Johnny's disappointment. Especially a disappointment whose roots went far deeper than his first marriage.

What Thea did deserve—just as she'd said all along—was a man willing to do whatever it took to keep her. Even if that meant opening up a part of himself he'd kept closed off for so long, he wasn't even sure what was in there anymore.

Because Thea was right—she wasn't Kat. Thea wouldn't

know how to hold back if her life depended on it. But both of them knew firsthand that marriages with one person doing more of the loving than the other didn't work. And friends or no, neither would this one, not in the long run.

So he knew what he had to do.

Naomi stuck around for about an hour, until Jess and Rach came with food and diapers and the car seat, which they'd use the next morning to go back to the house. Tonight, though, they'd stay put, in this insane little place Thea'd called home, letting the baby sleep between them in the funky blue bed where he'd most likely been conceived, where he'd been born.

And somewhere in there, while he watched his daughter exclaim over her new little brother, her husband standing behind her with his hands over *her* rounded belly, Johnny felt himself just…let her go. The instant he did, Rachel's eyes met his, like she knew. Then she smiled, wrinkling her nose, and Johnny thought, *It's okay, she's not going anywhere.*

Finally the house emptied out, leaving the three of them in peace to get to know each other.

For real, this time.

Johnny eased himself onto the mattress beside Thea, slipping one arm behind her shoulders as she held the baby, just staring and staring.

"All I want to do is look at him," she whispered, like she was afraid he might disappear if she talked too loudly.

"You got anything more pressing on your social calendar at the moment?"

"Guess not," she said, laughing a little, and it struck him, how much he'd miss that laughter if she left. How much he'd miss her. When he released a breath, a little more of the fear sloughed off with it. And the doubt.

With an achy tenderness like nothing he'd ever felt before, Johnny brought Thea's face around and kissed her, real slow and sweet, fully expecting the hundred questions in her eyes when he lifted his mouth from hers. But when not a single one of those questions fell from her lips, he said, "You done good, sweetheart. Real good."

"I didn't *do* anything," she said, her eyes dropping again to the little creature in her arms, sound asleep.

"Not true. *And* you did it without drugs."

"Oh, Lord…I did, didn't I?"

"And lived to tell the tale."

"Lived to know I never, ever want to do that again. Why put yourself through that kind of pain if you don't have to?"

And hadn't that been Johnny's motto for most of his life? Only now he realized he had a choice: He could hang on to his pain-filled past, like a bunch of moldy, dusty crap in a locked garage that you kept putting off sorting through and tossing; or he could finally open that damn garage door, do what he should've done a long time ago, and start fresh.

His silence had brought Thea's probing gaze back to his. Smiling a little, Johnny skimmed one finger across her cheek, then the baby's. "You probably want to get some sleep—"

"Johnny, for heaven's sake!"

Chuckling softly, he pulled her close to nestle his cheek in her hair. "Guess it's high time I told you how much I love you," he whispered, and she burst into tears. "Oh, hell, Thea, I—"

"No, no," she said, half laughing, half crying, batting at the air with her free hand, "it's just hormones. Okay, it's not just hormones, it's…" She wiped her eyes on the corner of the receiving blanket Rach'd brought over, then sniffed. "Took you long enough to admit it."

Frowning, Johnny reared back to look into her eyes.

"You knew?"

"Had a pretty good idea. But good Lord, were you fighting it or what?"

"I was scared, honey," Johnny said, gathering her in his arms again. "Scared I'd screw it up. That—" He swallowed.

"That I'd abandon you, too?"

"Yeah," he breathed out.

"I'm not that stupid," she said, smiling when Johnny took the baby from her so she could skootch down farther into the pillows.

"I'm crazy about you, *mi vida.* Hell, I'm even learning to love those damn dogs of yours. What?" he said when she tilted her head back again.

"What's with the Spanish all of a sudden?"

"It means 'my life.'"

"I know what it means—"

"It's what Andy and Maria called each other. And it's true. You *are* my life, Thea. Because before you, I wasn't really living."

She made a soft, strangled sound, then cuddled closer, letting the baby curl his tiny fingers around her index finger. "I'm crazy about you, too, Johnny. And I cannot tell you how good it feels to be able to say that and know it's not gonna bounce off a brick wall!"

Johnny smiled. "You know, I thought I had a pretty good handle on what obligation was. Turns out I had no idea."

"I don't know—seems to me you've been doing okay on that score."

"Oh, I had the letter of it down okay, I guess. Just not the soul." He paused. "Like my mother."

Wincing a little, Thea sat up, her hand on his arm. "Johnny…you don't have to talk about this if you don't want to. No, I'm serious," she added when he tried to protest. "Because right before I went into labor, I realized I've got no right to nag you about trusting me without affording you the same privilege. That if I love you, I have to respect your privacy." She leaned her head on his arm to touch the baby again. “Even if it drives me nuts.” Her eyes canted, meeting his. “Not that I don’t still stand by every single thing I said. But I can’t tell you how to work that out. Or when.”

“So…I could stop right now and you’d be okay with that?”

“Sure,” she said, averting her gaze, and Johnny chuckled.

“Yeah, well…I wouldn’t,” he said…and out it came. All of it. How his parents had only gotten married because *his* mom was pregnant, how although she’d treated him okay while his father was still around, the moment he split she turned against Johnny, blaming him for his father’s abandonment. That although the physical abuse had been sporadic, the emotional terrorism had been close to constant.

“Not a day passed,” he said quietly, shifting the baby slightly, “that she didn’t tell me I was worthless, or stupid, or a burden she’d never wanted. That I was the cause of all her troubles. That…if it hadn’t been for me, my father wouldn’t have left her.”

“Oh, Johnny…what a horrible, horrible thing to do to a child.”

No argument there, he thought, his chest tightening when the baby—so trusting, so innocent—scrunched up his tiny face, one little hand beating at the air. “The thing was, though…she was still my mom. I figured if she didn’t love me, it must be my fault somehow, that if I tried harder I could make her love me. Took a long time before I finally got it through my head that you can’t will somebody to love you. Either they do or they don’t.”

“But why didn’t you tell somebody what you were going through?”

“Funny thing,” he said, the pain and frustration still raw, even after all these years. “Tell a kid he’s unlovable long enough, that everything’s his fault, he starts to believe it. I honest to God didn’t think anybody else would care.”

“Until you started working for Andy?”

A rueful smile touched his lips. "You got any idea how long it takes an abused horse to trust again? You don't unlearn all that stuff overnight. Even living with Andy and Maria wasn't enough to shake loose the doubts, not really. So with Kat...I couldn't believe my good fortune, that somebody like her would take up with somebody like me. And when it fell apart, I figured it was because I hadn't measured up in some way. That I wasn't good enough." He made a dismissive, clicking sound with his tongue. "And...every time somebody left me, I felt abandoned all over again."

"I know," Thea said gently. "But those days are over. You are loved, Johnny. Not just by me, but by more people than you count. Because if anybody deserves it, it's you."

"You, too, sweetheart," Johnny whispered, leaning over to kiss her again, only to be interrupted when the baby started to whimper. Johnny laid him gently back in Thea's arms, where she confidently put the baby to her breast. Took the tyke all of one second to figure out what that thing was poking him in the cheek before he latched on.

"Yep, just like your daddy," Thea muttered, and Johnny laughed. Then she looked up at him, her eyes alight. "Jonathan Andrew," she said, lifting the baby slightly in case he missed her meaning.

Johnny's eyes stung. "You sure?"

"Oh, yeah. Just like I'm sure I'm ready to let go of this place," she said quietly, looking around. She met his gaze again, her eyes soft. Determined. Full of love. "Because I don't need two homes. And this one's served its purpose. Time to move on."

After that they sat in comfortable silence for some time, listening to the snow already dripping off the roof, the soft sounds of the baby's first meal, until Thea suddenly said, "You know, I may have thought Mama was off her rocker for always taking my dirtwad father back, but at least her only crime was loving too *much.*"

"Guess there's one apple that didn't fall real far from the tree."

"You are *not* saying I'm just like my mother."

"Not at all," Johnny said, hiding his smile. Then he looped one arm around her shoulders and said, "Will you marry me, Anthea Louise Benedict?"

"Can't. Already married."

"Anybody ever tell you you're a real pain in the butt?"

"And your point is?"

"My point," he whispered, "is that this time, it's my heart asking you to marry me. Not my head. Not because we should, or because it might be what's best for the baby, but because I can't imagine my life without you in it. If you're good with that."

Smiling broadly, Thea said, "Oh, I'm definitely good with that," and Johnny kissed his wife, tasting true freedom for the first time in his life.

* * * * *

Celebrate 60 years of pure reading pleasure with Harlequin® Books!

Harlequin Romance® is celebrating by showering you with DIAMOND BRIDES *in February 2009. Six stories that promise to bring a touch of sparkle to your life, with diamond proposals and dazzling weddings, sparkling brides and gorgeous grooms!*

Enjoy a sneak peek at Caroline Anderson's TWO LITTLE MIRACLES, available February 2009 from Harlequin Romance®.

'I'VE FOUND HER.'

Max froze.

It was what he'd been waiting for since June, but now—now he was almost afraid to voice the question. His heart stalling, he leaned slowly back in his chair and scoured the investigator's face for clues. 'Where?' he asked, and his voice sounded rough and unused, like a rusty hinge.

'In Suffolk. She's living in a cottage.'

Living. His heart crashed back to life, and he sucked in a long, slow breath. All these months he'd feared—

'Is she well?'

'Yes, she's well.'

He had to force himself to ask the next question. 'Alone?'

The man paused. 'No. The cottage belongs to a man called John Blake. He's working away at the moment, but he comes and goes.'

God. He felt sick. So sick he hardly registered the next few words, but then gradually they sank in. 'She's got *what?*'

'Babies. Twin girls. They're eight months old.'

'Eight—?' he echoed under his breath. 'They must be his.'

He was thinking out loud, but the P.I. heard and corrected him.

'Apparently not. I gather they're hers. She's been there since mid-January last year, and they were born during the summer—June, the woman in the post office thought. She was more than helpful. I think there's been a certain amount of speculation about their relationship.'

He'd just bet there had. God, he was going to kill her. Or Blake. Maybe both of them.

'Of course, looking at the dates, she was presumably pregnant when she left you, so they could be yours, or she could have been having an affair with this Blake character before...'

He glared at the unfortunate P.I. 'Just stick to your job. I can do the math,' he snapped, swallowing the unpalatable possibility that she'd been unfaithful to him before she'd left. 'Where is she? I want the address.'

'It's all in here,' the man said, sliding a large envelope across the desk to him. 'With my invoice.'

'I'll get it seen to. Thank you.'

'If there's anything else you need, Mr Gallagher, any further information—'

'I'll be in touch.'

'The woman in the post office told me Blake was away at the moment, if that helps,' he added quietly, and opened the door.

Max stared down at the envelope, hardly daring to open it, but when the door clicked softly shut behind the P.I., he eased up the flap, tipped it and felt his breath jam in his throat as the photos spilled out over the desk.

Oh, lord, she looked gorgeous. Different, though. It took him a moment to recognise her, because she'd grown her hair, and it was tied back in a ponytail, making her look younger and somehow freer. The blond highlights were gone, and it was back to its natural soft golden-brown, with a little curl in the end of the ponytail that he wanted to thread his finger through and tug, just gently, to draw her back to him.

Crazy. She'd put on a little weight, but it suited her. She looked well and happy and beautiful, but oddly, considering how desperate he'd been for news of her for the past year—one year, three weeks and two days, to be exact—it wasn't only Julia who held his attention after the initial shock. It was the babies sitting side by side in a supermarket trolley. Two identical and absolutely beautiful little girls.

* * * * *

When Max Gallagher hires a P.I. to find his estranged wife, Julia, he discovers she's not alone—she has twin baby girls, and they might be his. Now workaholic Max has just two weeks to prove that he can be a wonderful husband and father to the family he wants to treasure.